Praise for
THE WARDSTONE CHRONICLES

'. . . ideal for the reader who has outgrown
Harry Potter. Be warned, these books are
seriously scary . . . Beautifully produced and
consistenly surprising, the weird and wonderful
Wardstone Chronicles are an annual treat'
AMANDA CRAIG, THE TIMES

'Wonderfully dark' THE BOOKSELLER

'Teenage readers looking . . . for total fantasy should
hasten to Joseph Delaney's *The Spook's Apprentice*'
INDEPENDENT

'. . . evocative, spine-tingling'
THE TIMES

'This thrilling and terrifying book
should not be read after dark!'
PARENT NEWS

'Well-packaged as horror, this is the kind of
story that will catch readers – full of action
with the threat of dark and dreadful deeds'
BOOKS FOR KEEPS

How to Read Spook's Symbols

Boggarts

Beta for Boggart

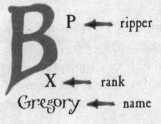

P ← ripper

Naturally
bound boggart

X ← rank

Gregory ← name

I – dangerous
X – hardly detectable

Artificially
bound boggart

Ghosts/Ghasts

I – dangerous
X – hardly detectable

X

Gregory

Witches

M – malevolent
B – benign
U – unaware

M

Gregory

Character profiles

Tom

Thomas Ward is the seventh son of a seventh son. This means he was born with certain gifts – gifts that make him perfect for the role of the Spook's apprentice. He can see and hear the dead and he is a natural enemy of the dark. But that doesn't stop Tom getting scared, and he is going to need all his courage if he is to succeed where twenty-nine others have failed.

The Spook

The Spook is an unmistakable figure. He's tall, and rather fierce looking. He wears a long black cloak and hood, and always carries a staff and a silver chain. Like his apprentice, Tom, he is left-handed, and is a seventh son of a seventh son.

For over sixty years he has protected the County from things that go bump in the night.

Alice

Tom can't decide if Alice is good or evil. She terrifies the local village lads, is related to two of the most evil witch clans (the Malkins and the Deanes) and has been known to use dark magic. But she was trained as a witch against her will and has helped Tom out of some tight spots. She seems to be a loyal friend, but can she be trusted?

Mam

Tom's mam has always known he would become the Spook's apprentice. She calls him her 'gift to the County'. A loving mother and an expert on plants, medicine and childbirth, Mam has always been a little different. Her origins in Greece remain a mystery. In fact, there are quite a few mysterious things about Mam . . .

WOLF FELL

WARD'S PEAK

Lane

Spook's
House

Woods

River

Bony
Lizzie's
House

THE WARDSTONE CHRONICLES

BOOK ONE:
THE SPOOK'S APPRENTICE

BOOK TWO:
THE SPOOK'S CURSE

BOOK THREE:
THE SPOOK'S SECRET

BOOK FOUR:
THE SPOOK'S BATTLE

BOOK FIVE:
THE SPOOK'S MISTAKE

BOOK SIX:
THE SPOOK'S SACRIFICE

BOOK SEVEN:
THE SPOOK'S NIGHTMARE

BOOK EIGHT:
THE SPOOK'S DESTINY

THE SPOOK'S STORIES
WITCHES

JOSEPH DELANEY

Illustrated by David Wyatt

RED FOX

THE SPOOK'S STORIES: WITCHES
A RED FOX BOOK 978 1 782 95251 0

First published in Great Britain by The Bodley Head,
an imprint of Random House Children's Publishers UK
A Random House Group Company
Bodley Head edition published 2009
First Red Fox edition published 2009
This edition published 2014

1 3 5 7 9 10 8 6 4 2

The Random House Group Limited supports the Forest Stewardship Council®
(FSC®), the leading international forest-certification organisation. Our books
carrying the FSC label are printed on FSC®-certified paper. FSC is the only
forest-certification scheme supported by the leading environmental organisations,
including Greenpeace. Our paper procurement policy can be found at
www.randomhouse.co.uk/environment

Set in 10.5/16.5pt Palatino by Falcon Oast Graphic Art Ltd.

Red Fox Books are published by Random House Children's Publishers UK,
61–63 Uxbridge Road, London W5 5SA

www.randomhousechildrens.co.uk
www.totallyrandombooks.co.uk
www.randomhouse.co.uk

Addresses for companies within The Random House Group Limited
can be found at: www.randomhouse.co.uk/offices.htm

THE RANDOM HOUSE GROUP Limited Reg. No. 954009

A CIP catalogue record for this book is available from the British Library.

Printed and bound in Great Britain by CPI Group (UK) Ltd, Croydon, CR0 4YY

for Marie

THE HIGHEST POINT IN THE COUNTY
IS MARKED BY MYSTERY.
IT IS SAID THAT A MAN DIED THERE IN A
GREAT STORM, WHILE BINDING AN EVIL
THAT THREATENED THE WHOLE WORLD.
THEN THE ICE CAME AGAIN, AND WHEN IT
RETREATED, EVEN THE SHAPES OF THE
HILLS AND THE NAMES OF THE TOWNS
IN THE VALLEYS CHANGED.
NOW, AT THAT HIGHEST POINT ON
THE FELLS, NO TRACE REMAINS OF WHAT
WAS DONE SO LONG AGO,
BUT ITS NAME HAS ENDURED.
THEY CALL IT –

THE WARDSTONE.

CONTENTS

MEG
SKELTON

This is a tale that must be told; a warning to those who might one day take my place. My name is John Gregory and I'm the local Spook; what now follows is the full and truthful account of my dealings with the witch Meg Skelton.

CHAPTER 1
THE FIGHT WITH THE ABHUMAN

F or five years my master, Henry Horrocks, had trained me as a spook, teaching me how to deal with ghosts, boggarts, witches and all manner of creatures from the dark. Now my apprenticeship was completed and I was fully qualified, still living at my master's Chipenden house and working alongside him to make the County a safer place.

Late in the autumn, an urgent message came from Arnside, to the north-west of the County, begging my old master and me to deal with an abhuman, a foul, monstrous creature that had brought terror to the district for far too long. Many families had suffered at its cruel hands and there had been many deaths and maimings.

Henry Horrocks's health had been deteriorating for quite some time, and three days before the message arrived he'd taken to his bed.

'You'll have to go on ahead, lad,' he told me, struggling for breath, his chest wheezing as he spoke. 'But take care – abhumans can be very strong. Keep it at bay as I've taught you, using your staff, then stab it through the forehead. If the job looks too dangerous, keep watch from a distance. As soon as I'm fit enough, I'll follow you north. Hopefully tomorrow . . .'

With those words we parted, and carrying my staff and bag, I set off for Arnside. Had I been going to face a witch, I would have borrowed my master's silver chain, but there were doubts about its effectiveness against abhumans, which have varying levels of resistance towards such tools of our trade as rowan wood, salt and iron. No – a blade was the best way to deal with such a creature.

I visited Arnside village and a few farms to gather as

much information as possible concerning the nature of what I faced and where I would find it. What I heard did little to boost my confidence. The creature was immensely strong and had attacked a farmer only a week earlier, ripping his head from his shoulders while the terrified milkmaid watched from her hiding place in the barn. After killing her unfortunate employer, the abhuman drank his blood, then tore the raw flesh from his bones with its teeth. It had now made its home in a tower and usually went hunting for prey soon after midnight. People for miles around were living in fear; no home was safe.

I came down into the forest at dusk. All the leaves had fallen and lay on the ground, rotten and brown. The tower was twice the height of the tallest trees, like a black demon finger pointing up at the grey County sky. A girl had been seen waving from its solitary window, frantically beckoning for aid. I'd been told that the creature had seized her for its own and now held her as its plaything, imprisoning her within those dank stone walls.

First I made a fire and sat gazing into its flames while I gathered my courage. It would be better to wait for Henry Horrocks to arrive; two of us would have a far greater chance against the creature. But despite his assurances I had no confidence that he would join me. His condition had been steadily worsening rather than improving. Besides, the creature would probably kill again this very night. It was my duty as a spook to deal with it before then; my duty to the people of the County.

Taking the whetstone from my bag, I sharpened the blade of my staff until my fingers could not touch its edge without yielding blood. Finally, just before midnight, I went to the tower and hammered out a challenge upon the wooden door with the base of my staff.

The creature came forth brandishing a great club and roared out in anger. It was a foul thing dressed in the skins of animals, reeking of blood. Almost seven feet tall, with a chest like a barrel, it was a truly formidable opponent. I am a spook and trained to

deal with creatures of the dark, and I was strong then and in my prime, but my courage faltered as it attacked me with a terrible fury.

At first I retreated steadily, but I released the blade from its recess in my staff and waited for my chance to counter-attack. Jabbing repeatedly at the beast to keep it at bay, I whirled to the left in a rapid spiral and drew it away from the tower into the trees. Twice that massive club smashed against tree trunks, missing my head by inches. Either blow would have shattered my skull like an eggshell.

But now it was my turn to attack. I whacked the creature hard on the side of the head, a blow that would have felled a village blacksmith, but it didn't even stagger. Then I managed to spear it deeply in the right shoulder so that, within moments, blood started to run down its bare arm and splatter onto the grass. That brought it to a halt and we faced each other warily.

As it bellowed in anger and prepared to attack again, I flicked my staff from my left hand to my right and drove it straight into the creature's forehead with all my strength. The blade went in deep and, with a gasp and then a terrible groan, the abhuman fell stone-dead at my feet.

I paused to catch my breath, looking down at the creature. I had no regrets about taking its life, for it would have killed again and again and would never have been sated.

It was then that the girl called out to me from the tower, her siren voice luring me up the stone steps. There, in the topmost room, I found her lying upon a bed of straw, bare-footed and bound fast with a long silver chain. With skin like milk and long fair hair, she was by far the prettiest woman that I had ever set eyes on. She told me that her name was Meg and pleaded to be released from the chain; her voice was so persuasive that my reason fled and the world spun about me.

No sooner had I unbound her from the coils of the chain than she fastened her lips hard upon mine. And so sweet were her kisses that I almost swooned away in her arms. It was a night that was to change my life. My first night with Meg.

I awoke to see sunlight streaming through the window, and spied the toes of Meg's shoes peeping out from under a chair in the corner of the room. They were pointy; pointy shoes. My heart sank within my chest. My master had warned me that pointy shoes were often a strong indication that the wearer might be a witch. Worse was to come, for as Meg dressed, I saw her back clearly for the first time and my blood froze cold within my veins. She was one of the lamia witches, and the mark of the serpent was upon her. Fair of face though she was, her spine was covered with green and yellow scales.

'Witch!' I cried, reaching for the silver chain. 'You're a witch!'

'I harm nobody!' she cried. 'Only those who wish *me* harm!'

'It's in your nature to practise deceit,' I said angrily.

'Once a witch, always a witch – your kind are not even human . . .'

I threw the chain that had previously bound her, and the long hours I'd spent casting against the practice post in the Chipenden garden paid off. The chain dropped over her head and shoulders, binding her fast so that she could neither walk, speak nor move her arms. Filled with anger at her deceit, I carried her, thus bound, back to Chipenden – where a terrible shock awaited me.

CHAPTER 2
HARBOURING A WITCH

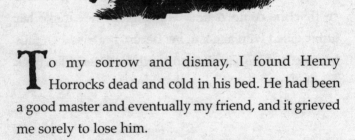

To my sorrow and dismay, I found Henry Horrocks dead and cold in his bed. He had been a good master and eventually my friend, and it grieved me sorely to lose him.

Leaving the witch safely bound, I buried my master at the edge of the local churchyard. Although a spook is not permitted to be interred in holy ground, no doubt some priest might have been persuaded to pray over his body, but Henry Horrocks had already told me that he didn't want that. He had lived a blameless, hard-working life defending the County against the dark, and felt capable of finding his own way through the mists of Limbo to the light.

That taken care of, it was time to deal with the witch. First I dug a pit for her in the eastern garden, then had the local mason and blacksmith construct its lid, a stone rim with thirteen iron bars. Once she was in the pit, I would drag the lid into position.

By now my anger had abated somewhat. I had left Meg chained to the side of the house, where she had been soaked to the skin by a heavy downpour of rain. She looked a pitiful sight, but despite her bedraggled appearance her beauty still captivated me. My heart lurched with pity and I had to harden my resolve.

When I released her from the chain, she struggled so fiercely that I barely overcame her and was forced to pull her by her long hair through the trees towards the pit, while she ranted and screamed fit to wake the dead. It was still raining hard and she slipped on the wet grass, but I carried on, dragging her along the ground, though her bare arms and legs were scratched by brambles. It was cruel but it had to be done.

We reached the edge of the pit, but when I started

to tip her over the edge, she clutched at my knees and began to sob pitifully.

'Please!' she cried. 'Spare me. I can't live like that – not trapped down there in the dark!'

'You're a witch and that's where you belong,' I told her. 'Be grateful you're not suffering a worse fate—'

'Oh, please, please, John, think again. Can I help it that I was born a witch? Despite that, I never hurt others unless they threaten me. Remember what we said to each other last night? How we felt? Nothing's changed. Nothing's changed at all. Please put your arms around me again and forget this foolishness.'

I stood there for a long time, full of anguish, about to topple over the edge myself – until, at last, I made a decision that changed my life.

She was a lamia witch and such creatures have two forms. Meg appeared to be in the domestic, near-human shape rather than the feral one, in which form the creatures become savage killers. So perhaps she spoke the truth. Maybe she did only use her strength in self-defence.

There was hope for her, I thought. So why not give her a chance?

I helped her to her feet and wrapped my arms about her and we both wept. My love for her was so sudden and all-consuming that my heart almost burst through my chest. How could I put her into the pit when I loved her better than my own soul? It was her eyes that captivated me: they were the most beautiful I'd ever seen – along with her voice, which was sweeter and more melodious than any siren song.

I begged her forgiveness, and then we turned together and, hand in hand, walked away from the pit, back towards the house that now belonged to me.

It was a fateful night and sometimes, despite my faith in free will and my firm belief that, minute by minute, second by second, we shape our own futures, it does seem to me that some things are meant to be. For had Henry Horrocks still been alive on my return, Meg would certainly have gone into a pit.

But I was captivated by Meg and she became the

love of my life. Beauty is a terrible thing: it binds a man tighter than a silver chain about a witch.

We lived happily together for almost a month in my Chipenden house, Meg and I. My fondest memories are of the times we sat together on the bench in the western garden, holding hands and watching the sun go down.

However, things soon started to go wrong. Unfortunately, Meg was very strong-willed, and against my wishes she insisted on visiting the village shops. Her tongue was as sharp as a barber's razor, and right from the start she began to have lively arguments with some of the village women. These disagreements had small beginnings: one woman pushed in front of Meg in a shop, as if she wasn't there. Another called her an 'incomer', and she sensed hostility from all the women to an outsider who was certainly prettier than any of them. A few of these disputes quickly developed into bitter feuds. No doubt there was spite on both sides.

'Meg, let me do the shopping,' I suggested to her. 'You're drawing too much attention to yourself. If it wasn't for me being a spook and you living at my house, they'd have already accused you of being a witch. You'll end up in the dungeons at Caster Castle if you're not careful!' I warned.

'I can take care of myself, John,' she replied, 'as you well know. Would you want me to be confined to this house and garden just because some shrews in the village insist on making trouble? No, I must fight my own battles!'

Eventually, being a witch, Meg resorted to witchcraft against her enemies. She did no serious harm to the women. One suffered nasty boils all over her body; another exceptionally house-proud woman who worshipped cleanliness had recurring infestations of lice and a plague of cockroaches in her kitchen.

At first the accusations were little more than whispers. Then one woman spat at Meg in the street and received a good hard slap for her discourtesy.

It would probably have stopped at that, but unfortunately she was the sister of the parish constable.

One morning the bell rang at the withy-trees crossroads and I went down to investigate. Instead of the poor boggart-haunted farmer that I had been expecting, the stout red-faced parish constable was standing there, truncheon in his belt and hands on his hips.

'Mr Gregory,' he said, his manner proud and pompous, 'it has come to my attention that you are harbouring a witch. The woman, known as Margery Skelton, has used witchcraft to hurt some good women of this parish. She has also been seen at midnight, under a full moon, gathering herbs and dancing naked by the pond at the edge of Homeslack Farm. I have come to arrest her and demand that you bring her to this spot immediately!'

'Meg no longer lives with me!' I said. 'She's gone to Sunderland Point to sail for her homeland, Greece.'

It was a lie of course, but what could I do? There was

no way I was going to deliver Meg into his hands. The man would take her north to Caster – where, no doubt, she'd eventually hang.

I could see that the parish constable wasn't satisfied, but there was little he could do about it immediately. Being a local, he knew not to enter my garden for fear of what he might find there. Generations of spooks had lived and worked at Chipenden, and the villagers believed the house and its surroundings were haunted by denizens of the dark. So he went away with his tail between his legs. I had to keep Meg away from the village from that day forth. It proved difficult and was the cause of many arguments between us, but there was worse to come.

Egged on by his sister, the constable went to Caster and made a formal complaint to the High Sheriff there. Consequently they sent a young constable with a warrant to arrest Meg. I was told about his imminent arrival by the village blacksmith, so I was ready. I needed to get Meg away as quickly as possible.

My former master had bequeathed another house

to me: it lay on the edge of brooding Anglezarke Moor. I had visited it just once and found little about it to my taste. Now it could be put to good use. In the dead of night, very late in the autumn, Meg and I journeyed to Anglezarke and set up home there.

It was a bleak place, wet and windy, with the winter threatening long months of ice and snow. The house had no garden and was built in a ravine, right back against a sheer rocky crag that kept it in shadow for most of the day. It was big, with ten bedrooms, including an attic, and a deep cellar; but even though I lit fires in every room, it was cold and damp – not a place where I could safely store books. However, we made the best of it and were happy for a while. But then there was an unexpected development that made my life much more difficult.

Unbeknown to me, Meg had written to her sister, giving her our new address. When the reply arrived, she became agitated. I found her pacing up and down in the kitchen, the letter clutched to her chest.

'What ails you, woman?' I demanded.

'It's my sister, Marcia,' she admitted at last. 'Unless we help, she'll be killed for sure. Can she come here to us?'

I groaned inside. Her sister? Another lamia witch!

'Where is she now?'

'Far to the north beyond the boundaries of the County. She's being hidden and protected but it can't go on for much longer or those who guard her will be in danger themselves. There's a quisitor in the area and he's already growing suspicious. A thorough search is being carried out. Please say she can come here,' Meg begged. 'Please do. She's my only relative in the whole world . . .'

Quisitors worked for the Church, and hunted down and burned witches. I had no love for such men – they would burn a spook too if they got the chance. Often they were corrupt and colluded with jealous neigh-bours to burn women who were totally innocent of witchcraft. Afterwards they confiscated their land and grew rich.

'She can come for a while until the danger is over,' I

23

said, relenting at last. I was too much in love with Meg to deny her anything.

Meg wrote back, and later that week a reply came. Her sister was travelling to Anglezarke by coach. We were to meet her on the Bolton road at the foot of the moor.

'She's coming by night,' Meg said. 'It'll be safer for her that way . . .'

CHAPTER
3
JUST A PUSSYCAT

So it was that just after midnight we waited shivering at the crossroads for the coach that would bring her sister to stay with us. There was still snow on the ground, but there had been no fresh falls for over three days so I was reasonably confident that the road would be open. At last, in the distance, we saw the coach approaching, the breath of the team of six horses steaming in the cold night air.

I waited for Marcia to alight from the coach, but instead, the driver and his mate jumped down and began to unfasten the ropes that bound something large to the back. They carried it towards us and laid it at our feet. It was a black coffin . . .

Without a word the two men climbed back up onto the coach; then the driver cracked his whip, brought the horses about and off they went again, back the way they'd come. I felt cold inside. Colder than the air freezing my forehead and cheeks.

'Don't tell me this is what I think it is . . .' I said softly.

'My sister is inside. How else could she have got here undetected?'

'She's feral, isn't she?'

Meg nodded.

'Why didn't you tell me?'

'Because you would never have allowed her to come here . . .'

Cursing under my breath, I helped Meg drag the coffin back up the slope towards the house. Beautiful though she was, Meg was extremely strong, and once back in the house she wasted no time in tearing off the lid with her bare hands.

I stood back, my staff at the ready. 'Can you control her?' I asked.

'She's just a pussycat.' Meg smiled, stepping back to allow Marcia to scuttle from the open coffin.

It was the first time I'd seen a lamia in the feral form. My master had described them to me and I'd read entries from books in the Chipenden library, but nothing could have prepared me for the actual thing.

Marcia was far from human in shape: she balanced herself, as if ready to spring, on four thin limbs which ended in large hands; each finger had a long claw. Her back was covered in green and yellow scales and her hair was long and greasy, falling over her shoulders as far as the ground. Her face, which looked up at us each in turn, was like something out of a nightmare, with gaunt features and heavy-lidded eyes.

Marcia first took up residence in the attic, and this worked well enough for a week or so. A feral lamia can summon birds to her side, where they wait in thrall, unable to fly off, until she finally devours them. The attic had a big skylight and I would hear the birds gathering on the roof; then their cries of terror as she pulled off their wings and, too late, they realized they were food for a lamia.

Then there were the rats. She could summon them too. I would hear them squealing in excitement as they climbed up the drainpipes, finally using the same route as the birds and dropping through the skylight to scamper across the floorboards. Every evening I would hear Marcia scuttling about as she chased them, and Meg would look up from her weaving and give me a warm smile.

'She likes a juicy rat, that sister of mine. But the chase is as good as the eating!'

Every week Meg would bring Marcia raw meat from the butcher's to supplement her diet. She looked after her sister well, regularly sweeping the attic floor clean of feathers and rat-skins. I wasn't happy, but what could I do? I didn't want to lose Meg. And I reasoned that a feral lamia was better off safe in the attic of my house than roaming free and threatening the County.

But then, one dark moonless night, Marcia got out through the skylight, went up onto the moor and killed a sheep. There was a bloody trail leading back to the house where she'd dragged the carcass behind her. Luckily a fresh fall of snow before dawn obscured the tracks so the farmer was none the wiser. I imagine he put the loss down to wolves or the wild dogs that sometimes ran in packs on Anglezarke Moor during the winter.

Meg gave her sister a good talking to and told me that she'd promised never to do it again.

It was just a few weeks later that Marcia first came downstairs . . .

I had been sitting next to Meg, facing the fire, when I heard unexpected sounds on the stairs: the clip-clop of shoes. I turned and saw Marcia peering at us from the doorway. It was as if a savage animal, a predator, had suddenly dressed itself in human clothes; a creature that was breathing too rapidly and noisily and still hadn't learned how to stand properly.

'Come here, sister, and sit beside us. Warm yourself at the fire,' Meg invited.

I was shocked by the change in her appearance.

Lamias are slow shape-shifters, and the weeks Marcia had lived at the house and the long hours she'd spent in the company of her sister had altered her form significantly towards the domestic. She was wearing a pair of her sister's pointy shoes and one of her dresses: the garment's hem was knee-length and cut away at the shoulders, and I could see how Marcia's arms and legs had fleshed out. Her hair had been cut neatly too, and her long deadly claws were the only visible aspect of the feral that remained. Her face was almost fully human, with a wild, savage beauty.

Marcia sat herself down and looked at me out of the corners of her eyes; she licked her lips before giving me a twisted smile.

'We could share him, sister, couldn't we? A man between us. Why not?'

'He's mine!' Meg retorted. 'I don't share my man with anyone – not even my sister!'

I think that was what hardened Meg against Marcia; what spurred her to alert me to danger in the middle of the night.

'Marcia's not in the attic!' she told me breathlessly. 'She's gone out onto the moor, looking for food.'

'Not another sheep,' I groaned, swinging my legs out over the edge of the bed and starting to pull on my boots. It seemed that Marcia, despite her changed appearance, still had much of the feral lamia's inner urges.

'No. It's worse than that. Far worse. She's after a child. One she spied at the farm when she killed that sheep. I thought I'd talked her out of it!'

'How long has she been gone?'

'A few minutes at most. I heard a noise on the roof and went up to the attic and found her missing.'

Marcia's tracks were easy enough to follow across the snow-clad moor. Meg went with me, offering to help as best she could.

'If she kills a child, they'll find her eventually. She'll never get away with that and we'll have to move again,' Meg complained.

'That may well be true, but we should be thinking of the poor child. The child and her family!' I retorted angrily, increasing my pace. Would we be too late? I wondered with sinking heart.

The footprints led through the farm gate and into the yard. Then we saw Marcia crouching in the shadow of the barn, looking up at a window – no doubt the bedroom of her intended prey. I breathed a sigh of relief. We could still save the child.

'No, sister, you're going too far!' Meg called out, keeping her voice low so as not to disturb the household. 'Come back with us now!'

But blood-lust held Marcia in its grip; she was beyond words. She hissed at us, then looked up at the bedroom again. Suddenly she kicked off her pointy shoes, surged forward and scampered straight up the sheer wall of the house, her finger- and toenails gouging into the stone.

She smashed the glass with her left fist, then seized the window frame and plucked the whole thing, wood and remaining glass panes, from the wall and hurled it down into the yard, where it fell with a tremendous crash. She climbed into the bedroom and I heard a child cry out with fear. The next moment she jumped out through the window again, down into the yard, and landed facing me, carrying the child under her arm. It was more baby than toddler and it was screaming its lungs out.

'Give the child to me, Marcia!' I commanded, my left hand targeting her with the blade of my staff, my right reaching out towards the baby.

She hesitated, and maybe she would have done as I instructed. But all at once the farmer burst out of the front door brandishing a big stick, his wife at his heels wailing as loud as a banshee. He went straight for Marcia, but she swiped him with the fingers of her free hand, the talons laying open his forehead to the bone. He fell to his knees, blood running into his eyes, while his wife screamed even louder and started tearing at her hair.

Seizing her chance, Marcia raced off across the farmyard and I immediately gave chase. She started to climb, heading up towards the moor tops. She

33

seemed to be pulling ahead even though I was running as fast as I could. I glanced back. Meg was quickly catching up with me. When she drew level, I shouted out angrily.

'If your sister kills that baby, I'll put my blade through her heart! Do something now or she's dead!' I warned, and I meant every word.

In response Meg began to surge ahead of me. I was slowing because of the deepening snow, but she was starting to close on her sister. I lost sight of them as they passed beyond the brow of one of the lower slopes. When they came into view again, there was a series of blood-curdling yells and screams.

They were fighting: clawing, biting and scratching so that blood sprayed out onto the snow. But where was the baby?

To my relief, I saw that it lay on the ground to one side, still crying loudly. My first instinct was to pick the child up and get it away from the danger of that furious fight. But then the two witches broke apart and I saw my chance.

With a flick of my wrist, I cast my silver chain towards Marcia; it was the one I'd inherited from my master – though I also had the one that had once bound Meg in the abhuman's tower. It was a good shot and it dropped over Marcia's head and bound her tightly, bringing her down into the snow.

Meg wiped the blood from her face, went over to pick up the child and started to whisper in its ear. I don't know what she said, but it was effective: within seconds it became silent, closed its eyes and nestled against her neck.

I hefted the bound Marcia into position over my left shoulder and headed back towards the farm. When we arrived, the mother cried louder than ever at being re-united with her baby, but they were tears of joy.

'Thank you! Thank you! I never thought I'd see my little girl again!' she said between sobs. 'My poor husband though – he'll be scarred for life!'

I wondered how grateful she'd be if she knew that

I'd been harbouring her baby's abductor in my own house? So with Meg walking silently at my side, I trudged back to my house, deep in thought. Once inside I told Meg what I intended.

'Down in the cellar there are graves and pits ready for boggarts and witches. So far they're all empty. My master, Henry Horrocks, had them prepared for the work he was doing locally. But after staying here for a while he decided that he didn't like this house, so they've never been used—'

'No! Please, John, don't put my sister in a pit. Don't do that . . .'

'I'll give her just one chance to avoid a pit, and one chance only. There are rooms on the upper levels of the cellar. She can stay in one of them – she'll be comfortable enough there. The iron gate on the cellar steps will give us extra security, so effectively she'll be sealed behind that gate and the neighbourhood will be safe.'

So that's what we did. A lamia has more resistance to iron than other witches, but the gate was very strong;

Marcia was in a secure place. Of course, Meg insisted on seeing her sister every day. They chatted in her room below the gate, and Meg often took her fresh meat and offal from the butcher. Marcia couldn't summon birds down there, but she ate a lot of rats – as I could see from all the skins Meg had to clear up.

The winter moved on and the days began to lengthen. I did a few jobs locally, including moving on a troublesome hall-knocker boggart and slaying a ripper with salt and iron. I realized that there was a lot of work to be done on Anglezarke Moor, but Chipenden also needed my help. Could I leave Meg here while I paid the village and its surroundings a short spring visit?

Eventually the decision was made for me, but in a way I didn't expect. It began in a similar fashion to the difficulties in Chipenden. A few words were exchanged between Meg and the local women. This time the constable didn't get involved because the people of Adlington had a strong sense of community and believed in sorting things out for themselves.

Meg still liked to go shopping, but I'd employed the local odd-job man, Bill Battersby, to bring me bulky supplies of potatoes and other vegetables up from the village to save her the trouble of carrying them. It was he who gave me warning of what was happening. To begin with it was nothing that I hadn't heard before: accusations of using curses – a woman suffering night-terrors; another too afraid to venture beyond her own front door. But then there was something new . . .

'She's after someone's husband. The villagers won't stand for that. Your Meg has gone too far!' Battersby warned.

'What do you mean? Make yourself clear!' I demanded, my heart already torn by his words. I knew precisely what he meant but couldn't bring myself to believe it.

'She's taken a fancy to Dan Crumbleholme, the village tanner. His wife, Dolly, spied them together. And there are reports that they've been seen kissing behind the tannery. Folks won't stand for it. They think she's used witchcraft to turn his head. If it happens again . . .'

I sent Battersby away with bitter words, still unable to believe that Meg would betray me by seeing another man. But I'd noticed that she'd taken to shopping later, when the sun was about to go down – something I could see no reason for. So the following afternoon I resolved to follow her.

I noticed that she had put on a pair of pointy shoes that she'd only bought the previous week. It was the first time she'd worn them and I remember thinking how attractively they set off her ankles. I kept my distance but was always in danger of being detected. A seventh son of a seventh son has a certain immunity against the powers of a witch, but Meg was exceptionally strong and I had to be vigilant.

Meg did her shopping, being the last customer at each shop she visited, and I began to feel better. No doubt she just shopped late to avoid the throng of local women and the opportunity for quarrels and disputes. But my relief was short-lived. She went to the tannery last of all. Worse, rather than knocking at the front door, which was already locked for the night, she went to the rear of the premises.

I didn't wait long before following her. I had hardly gone round the corner when the back door slammed and I saw Meg walking towards me.

'What are you up to, Meg?' I demanded.

'Nothing. Nothing at all,' she protested. 'I wanted some soft leather to stitch myself a new bag, that's all. The shop was shut but I knocked on the back door and Dan was kind enough to take my order even though his business has just shut for the night.'

I didn't believe her. She seemed flustered, which was unusual for Meg. We quarrelled bitterly, and following the heat of our exchange, a coldness came between us to rival that of the winter top of Anglezarke Moor. It persisted, and three days later, despite my protests, Meg went shopping again.

This time the village women resorted to violence. Over a dozen of them seized her in the market square. Bill Battersby told me later that she'd fought with fists like a man, but also scratched like a cat, almost blinding the ringleader of the women. Finally they struck her down from behind with a cobblestone and, once felled, she was bound tightly with ropes.

Only a silver chain can hold a witch for long, but they rushed her down to the pond and, after breaking the ice with stones, threw her into the deep cold water. If she drowned, they would accept that she was innocent of witchcraft; if she floated they'd have the satisfaction of burning her.

Meg did float, but face down, and after five minutes or so became very still in the water. The women were satisfied that she had drowned and didn't really have the stomach for burning her anyway. So they left her where she was.

It was Battersby who pulled her out of the pond. By rights she should have been dead, but Meg was incredibly tough. To his amazement, she soon began to twitch and splutter, coughing up water onto the muddy bank. He brought her back to my house across the back of his pony. She looked a sorry sight, but in hours she was fully recovered and soon started to plot her revenge.

I'd already thought long and hard about what needed to be done. I could cast her out; let her take her own chances in the world. But that would have broken my heart, because I still loved her. And I had to make allowances because it wasn't all Meg's fault. You see, she was an exceptionally pretty woman and it was natural that men should be attracted to her. The temptations for her were consequently greater than for most women, I told myself.

My knowledge of a special herb tea seemed to be the answer. It is possible to administer this to keep a witch in a deep sleep for many months. If the dose is reduced, she can even walk and talk – though it impairs the memory, making the witch forget her knowledge of the dark arts. So this was the method I decided to use.

It was very difficult to get the dosage right, and painful to see Meg so docile and mild, her fiery spirit (something that had attracted me to her in the first place) now subdued. So much so that, at times, she seemed a stranger to me. The worst time of all was when I decided to leave her alone in my Anglezarke house and returned to Chipenden for the summer. It had to be done lest the law catch up with her. There was still a danger that she might be hanged at Caster. So I locked her in a dark room off the cellar steps in so deep a trance that she was hardly breathing.

'Farewell, Meg,' I whispered into her ear. 'Dream of the garden at Chipenden where we were so happy. I'll see you in the autumn.'

As for her sister, Marcia, despite my former promise to Meg, I hired a mason and smith and had her bound in a pit in the cellar. I had no choice. I could not take the risk that she might eventually break through the iron gate. Without human companionship or contact with a domestic lamia, she would slowly shift her shape until she became feral again. And she wouldn't starve. She would never run out of rats – they could always be relied on.

I left for Chipenden with a heavy heart. Although I'd

experimented through the winter, I still worried whether or not I'd got Meg's dose of herb tea right. Too much and she might stop breathing; too little and she could wake up alone in that dark cell with many long weeks to wait until my return. So I spent our enforced separation riddled with sorrow and anxiety.

Fortunately I had calculated the dosage correctly and returned late the following autumn just as Meg was beginning to stir. It was hard for her, but at least she didn't hang, and the County was spared the harm she could have inflicted.

But a lesson must be learned from this, one that my apprentices should note carefully. A spook should never become romantically involved with a witch; it compromises his position and draws him dangerously close to the dark. I have fallen short in my duty to the County more than once, but my relationship with Meg Skelton was my greatest failing of all. This is a tale that had to be told and I'm glad the telling is over.

Always beware a woman who wears pointy shoes!

DIRTY DORA

My name is Dirty Dora Deane and I'm a dead witch.

Some call me Dirty because I spit thick slimy gobs of spittle to mark my territory. But I'm bad, not mad; have a reason for all I do. When I sniff that spit, I know I'm home and safe in the dell. Sniff it in the dark, I can, when I'm crawling back on my hands and knees.

Although I'm cold and dead now, and live under the rotting leaves in Witch Dell, I'm still strong enough to leave it and I want to tell my tales while I still can. Most nights I hunt for blood, but once or twice a week I go back to our cosy cottage, where my sister, Aggy, still lives. We chat together about the old times while my damp clothes steam in front of the fire; then, after Aggy has combed the beetles out of my hair, I spend a bit of time jotting down my memories. It's not easy because I find it difficult to remember what happened and I want to get it all down before it's all gone out of my mind – or I can't write no more. Don't know which will happen first. Never can tell with us dead witches. Sometimes the mind goes completely. Then again, it could be my hands that drop off so that I can't hold a pen. More than one dead witch crawls round the dell with pieces of her body missing. One ain't even got a head!

Now I only remember three things properly. Three chunks – that's all. The rest has gone.

CHAPTER 1
MY SABBATHS

I'll start by telling you about my sabbaths. The ones I enjoyed as a girl and a young woman.

The four main ones are Candlemas, Walpurgis, Lammas and Halloween. They're the nights when the Pendle witches meet. Not together, mind. The different clans don't see eye to eye; they gather in different places. We Deanes usually meet on the outskirts of our village and build a big fire. The thirteen members of the coven form a circle around it, warming their hands. Other witches from the clan stand further back, according to their age and power.

We kill a lamb first, slitting its throat and covering our hands and faces with its warm blood. Once its carcass has been thrown into the fire, we start with curses, shrieking them up into the sky to fly out towards our enemies or make their bodies wither and rot. Exciting, it is. Loved that more than anything when I was young.

But Halloween was always my favourite sabbath because that was when the Fiend sometimes paid a visit. Got lots of names, he has. Some call him Old Nick, but people who ain't witches usually call him the Devil.

Didn't stay long, but it was good just to get a glimpse of him. Most witches want to see the Fiend at least once in their lives. Big, he was. Very big, with a tail, hooves and lovely glossy black hair all over his body. And what a lovely stink he gave out – ranker than a tom-cat. He'd appear right in the middle of the flames, and the coven members would reach out their hands to touch and stroke him, not caring about burning their arms.

I remember the night it all went wrong though. The night when an enemy stole into our gathering. Nobody saw it coming. Nobody sniffed it out. The Fiend had just appeared in the flames and all our eyes were on *him*, not on what was dashing out of the darkness straight towards the fire.

It was a wild woman, her hair flying behind her as she ran. She carried three blades – one in each hand, the third gripped between her teeth. She burst right through to the edge of the flames before anyone could stop her, and threw a blade straight at the Fiend. I heard him scream, a shriek that split the sky above with forked lightning and made the stones groan beneath our feet.

But she wasn't satisfied with that. Twice more she threw her blades. I wasn't close enough to see, but they told me later that all three reached their target: the first one stuck in his chest, the second in his throat, and the third went up to the hilt in the left cheek of his hairy arse. The latter would have been the worst for sure, but he turned away at the last moment.

Why he didn't kill her on the spot nobody knows – certainly not we Deanes. The Fiend simply vanished, and the fire died down and went out in an instant, plunging us all into darkness. That was how the mad knifewoman made her escape.

We raked three blades out of the embers of the fire. Each one was tipped with silver. We used our best scryers, but we couldn't find out who the madwoman was or where she'd gone. She'd cloaked herself in powerful magic.

Later we sent assassins after her, three in all, over the space of a few days. Not one of them came back, and then the trail went cold and even the best trackers couldn't find her. The Fiend didn't appear to us for five years after that. It was a bad time. Really bad. Our magic was weak or didn't work at all, and some of our coven died of wasting diseases. They say it was the Fiend taking his revenge on us because we hadn't taken enough precautions against an intruder; we hadn't kept him safe.

Why she did it nobody knows – at least, perhaps some do but, if so, they ain't saying. Got a glimpse of her face as she passed me sprinting towards the fire.

She was young, hardly more than a girl . . . somehow, I felt I knew her. Seen her somewhere before. Almost had her name. Almost. It was on the tip of my tongue . . .

They were good times until then. I miss being part of that big happy group. Most of all I miss the cursing and seeing the Fiend. Who knows, if I'd lived long enough, I might have become one of the coven and got to stroke the Fiend myself. But that wasn't to be. The mad girl spoiled all that.

And there was something else. Didn't see it coming, but my life was almost over.

CHAPTER 2
MY DOOM

We are all fated. All doomed. What is written will be. We witches can sniff out the future, see dangers approaching. But few of us see our own doom coming. I certainly didn't . . .

Over seventy years ago, even before my mother was born, a quisitor called Wilkinson arrived in Pendle. Wanted to deal with the clans once and for all, so he brought priests, wardens and thirty special constables. And they were all armed to the teeth and keen to kill witches.

Made his base in Downham, he did, and started to arrest suspected witches from all three clan villages – Goldshaw Booth, Roughlee and Bareleigh. Not all clan members are witches though, and he tried to sort them out using different tests. He swam a dozen of them. Three drowned and another died of fever afterwards. Another three sank but were dragged out barely alive. The five who floated were tried, found guilty and hanged at Caster Castle. But swimming never works, and only one of them was really a witch. Not that it bothered Wilkinson much anyway. He was a nasty, greedy man. He seized their houses and possessions, sold them and kept the money.

After that he arrested lots more – mainly Malkins. Tested them with a bodkin this time; jabbed its sharp blade into their flesh until he found what he called 'the Devil's Mark', a place where he said they couldn't feel any pain. All nonsense of course, but they say that he enjoyed his work.

However, the clans weren't going to stand for that. Not them. So they banded together in a temporary truce and collected their dead. Buried them under the loam in Witch Dell with the others. Somehow Wilkinson and his men were tricked into passing through the dell. Don't know how they did it. Nobody seems to remember that.

It happened after dark, as they were travelling back to Downham. The dead witches were lying in wait, desperate for blood.

Wilkinson survived, but over half his party were slaughtered. Their bodies were recovered later – but in broad daylight, of course, with the bright sun overhead. All the dead had been drained of blood and their thumb-bones were missing.

The quisitor was in fear for his own life, so he made a hasty retreat from the district. But they weren't finished with him yet, were they. The Malkin clan used a powerful curse, and within thirteen months every last one of Wilkinson's men was dead, including him. Some died in accidents; others just vanished from the face of the earth – probably victims of witch assassins. Wilkinson's own death was particularly horrible. His nose and fingers fell off and his ears turned black and withered away. Scared of dying but scared of living, he was too. So he tried to hang himself but failed when the rope gave way. Driven mad with pain, he drowned himself in a local pond. So the clans' revenge was complete. Didn't think anyone would ever try it again.

Became too sure of ourselves, we did. All of us – me included. Well, I paid the price for that and no mistake. Didn't see my own doom coming, did I?

One morning I was begging at a farm gate on the outskirts of Downham. This was the third time I'd been back in less than a week and I'd scared that old farmer good and proper – threatened to make his crops fail and his livestock be struck down with foot and mouth. The first time I'd just asked for eggs; the second, a leg of lamb; but this time I'd come for his hoard of coins.

Farmers are always moaning and crying poverty, but most of them have got something squirreled away. 'I want money this time,' I told him. 'Nothing less will do . . .'

'I have no money,' he protested. 'I can scarcely make

ends meet. You've already taken the food out of my children's mouths . . .'

'Ah, you have children,' I said, giving him a wicked grin. 'I do hope they thrive! How many have you?'

At that his hands began to shake and his bottom lip to tremble like a withered leaf in an autumn gale. I could tell that he really loved those children of his.

'Two girls,' he said, 'and another child on the way.'

'You're a bit old to be a father. Got a young wife, have you?'

There was a movement in the doorway and a woman came out into the late evening light and started to peg out her washing. She was less than half his age but a bit of a dumpling and not at all pretty.

'Give me your money or it'll be the worse for you,' I threatened.

The farmer shook his head, his expression a mixture of despair and defiance. He was on the fence now and didn't know which way to jump, so I made up his mind for him.

'Wouldn't want anything to happen to that little

defenceless unborn your wife's carrying in her belly, would you? And what about her? Is she strong? What if she were to die in childbirth? How would you manage this farm alone as well as raising young children?'

'Be off with you!' he cried, raising his stick.

'Give you a chance, I will. Be back tomorrow at the same time. Don't want all your money – I'm not greedy. Half will do. Have it ready or suffer the consequences!'

Should have sniffed out what was coming. A stinky wind blows from the future, but I didn't even get a whiff.

Next evening the old farmer was waiting for me at the gate but his hands were empty. Where was my bag of coins? I wondered angrily.

'Made a big mistake, you have!' I warned him, curling my lip. 'Got a nasty curse ready for you, old man. I'll make the flesh drop off your young wife's bones . . .'

He didn't reply. Not only that, he didn't even look

scared. Well, maybe just a bit nervous, but not what I'd expected. I opened my mouth to begin the curse, but suddenly heard footsteps behind, running towards me. I turned and saw half a dozen big men with clubs approaching, spread out in a big arc and cutting off any hope of escape.

Right! I'd show him. I leaped the gate and ran past the farmer towards the house. His wife was inside – and, even better, his children. I'd take them hostage; use them to make my escape. I slipped my sharp knife – the blade I used to take thumb-bones – down my sleeve into my left hand to be ready. Let 'em know I meant business. I'd almost reached the back door when I was brought to a sudden halt.

A man was standing just inside; behind him lurked another one holding a large stick. Swaggering confidently, they both came out into the yard in front of me. By then other men were climbing over the gate behind me, and within moments they'd surrounded me. I tried to fight, I really did. I spun and slashed at them with my knife, but there were too many of them and the blows they dealt were savage. One of the first knocked the knife from my hand; then they rained down on my back and shoulders. I crouched low, trying to cover my head, but they found it eventually. There was a flash of light and then darkness.

I was the first they captured that day. In the end five of us were tested down at the pond. By chance I'd chosen to beg from that farm on the very day that a witchfinder had called at Downham; the first such visit to Pendle by a quisitor since the days of Wilkinson. The farmer had gone to warn him and then they'd set their trap and awaited my return.

How come I chose that day and that place? It was my doom. It had been fated to happen.

Swimming is terrifying. We witches can't cross running water but lakes and ponds are usually no problem. I'd even been known to kneel at the water's edge and wash myself once in a while. Not in winter though – far too cold then. Dirt keeps out the winter chills.

But it's very different when your hands are tied to your feet. I was the third they swam that cold January afternoon. The first woman floated. She was just a clan member and lacked the craft, but that didn't bother them: dragged her out of the pond, they did, and threw her up into the back of a wagon.

The second one sank like a stone – and she was a real witch; one of the Malkins. The Fiend didn't bother to save her, did he? Told you swimming don't work. They took their time getting her out of the water. By the time they did she'd stopped breathing, so they chucked her body back into the pond, where it sank for a second time.

Then it was my turn. Two of them swung me back and forth before letting go. I hit the water hard. Was going to try and hold my breath, but that cold water was too much of a shock. I gasped and opened my mouth. The dirty water rushed in. I seemed to sink, but must have been floating face down. I could see the dead witch below me through the murk, hair drifting over her open mouth and bony nose, dead eyes staring up at me. I choked for a while but then it didn't hurt any more. Gave up, I did. I was going into the dark. Well, why not? I'm a witch. That's where I belong.

Next thing I knew, I was lying in the mud, pond water gushing out of my mouth. Then I was sick as a dog over one of the men's boots. Gave me a good kicking for that, he did, before bundling me into the back of the wagon.

They called three of us witches and rushed off towards Caster. Weren't going to risk the wrath of the clans this time, were they? Wanted to get us away from Pendle and into the safety of Caster Castle.

Thrown into a dark dungeon, I was. And all alone. Not that I wanted the company of the other two. One was a Mouldheel, the other a Malkin – clan enemies. Dark and damp, it was, down there, with water dripping from the ceiling and just a bed of filthy straw to lie on. They couldn't even leave me in peace to enjoy my misery though. Came for me at midnight. Dragged me along a corridor and into a room with a big wooden table. Clamped my wrists and chained my arms. Weren't satisfied with testing me once.

'Before we kill a witch, we have to be doubly sure she *is* one,' said the quisitor. 'We've used swimming. Now it's time for pricking!'

Really loved his work, that one. Matthew Carter was his name, and he smiled as he stuck that long pin into me. The more I groaned and flinched and shrieked, the more he loved it. I fainted more than once. Soon my body was hurting all over and I couldn't tell when he was jabbing me and when he'd stopped. Said he'd found the Devil's Mark then. True enough, I'd a birthmark just below my knee. About the same size as a copper coin, it was, and this was where he said the Devil had touched me; a place where the Fiend protected me and I couldn't feel pain. It was enough for him. I was proved a witch twice over.

They were going to execute us just after dawn – that's what he told me – and I spent the long night in that dungeon shivering with cold and fear. Couldn't face being burned. Not that. Please not that! The pain was supposed to be terrible. And a witch can't come back after burning. She has to stay in the dark for ever then.

They took us out into the yard at first light. It was a miserable morning with heavy drizzle falling out of a grey sky. I remember there were three seagulls on a nearby roof – one for each witch about to die. But then my spirits lifted because I saw what awaited us in the far corner of the castle yard. It wasn't a fire. It was a gallows. They were going to hang us. That meant I'd be able to come back . . .

Can't say it was pleasant though. Not nice to be swinging on a rope, panting for breath, with your face going purple and eyes bulging. That's the last thing I saw: the Mouldheel witch hanging next to me, gasping out her last breaths. Then my sight dimmed and everything went dark. All I could hear was my own heart thudding. At first it was going so fast that the thumps all merged into one. Then it grew tired. It was faltering . . . slowing . . . missing beats.

Funny thing, dying. Strange the last memories you have. I saw the madwoman run past me again on her way to throw her knives at the Fiend. Suddenly I recognized her. Knew her name! It was . . .

But then I died.

CHAPTER 3
MY REVENGE

The Deane clan collected my body from the castle yard and took it back to Pendle. They buried me in a shallow grave in Witch Dell and covered the bare earth with rotting leaves. Then they left me to enjoy my new existence.

I remember sensing something above, so I stretched up my arms into the chill night air. I sat up and my head burst through the covering of earth. The dell was lit with a silver light: I was looking up through the branches of a tree towards a yellow orb. It was the full moon. That was what first summoned me back to this world.

My next need was blood. Never had I felt so

hungry. I began to crawl through the dell, sniffing for prey. There were no humans within range but I soon caught a few juicy rats and a field mouse. The rats took the edge off my appetite. Very small, the mouse was, hardly a mouthful, but I couldn't remember anything tasting so delicious. I was a bone witch but had drunk blood before – though none tasting like that. It's so much better when you're dead. You don't need ordinary food any more. What good are potatoes and cooked meat to a dead stomach?

That food, little though it was, gave me strength. Now I could stand ... walk ... maybe even run? So how would I feel if I managed to catch a man, woman or child and drink human blood? Some dead witches ain't that strong and the most they can ever do is crawl. I felt sure I'd be one of the stronger ones.

So I slid under my covering of leaves again and lay on my back for a while, just my nose and eyes peeping up through them. Lying there, I suddenly noticed just how much my head itched. I kept having to scratch it. That's the problem with spending so much time close to the ground and hiding under dead leaves. Things get into your hair and make their homes there.

You get lots of time to think when you're a dead witch. And my first thoughts were of revenge. At first I decided just to kill that farmer and his dumpling wife; the children would be really juicy. But that would be too easy. There was someone else I really owed for what had happened. Matthew Carter had tortured and murdered me; brought my happy life to an end. I wouldn't enjoy sabbaths no more; would never get to stroke the Fiend.

Deserved the same back, he did, and more. But how could I get to him? I now knew he was based in Caster. It was a long way there – could be done, but surely there had to be a better way . . .

Didn't take me long to work it out, so I set out for Downham right away. I was going to have a serious talk with that old farmer.

I still wasn't as strong as I'd have liked but I made my way slowly north, keeping Pendle Hill to my left. Just before dawn I managed to catch a couple of rats and settled myself down under a hedge to while away the daylight hours.

It was long after midnight the following night before I arrived at the boundary of his farm. The first thing I did was kill one of his pigs. It was a small plump pink thing, and it squealed almost until the moment it died. That started the farm dogs barking: must have been chained up or they'd have caught my scent. Pity, that. I could have managed to drain a dog or two. But I have to tell you that pig blood is quite tasty. Next best thing to draining a human.

That little squealer made me feel a lot stronger. I walked up to the front of the farmhouse and pulled the door right off its hinges. Somewhere above, a child started to cry; it was soon joined by another, and it wasn't long before the old farmer came to the top of the stairs in his nightshirt, the stub of a candle in his trembling hand. He saw me standing in the open doorway, gave a cry of terror and ran back into the bedroom. I heard him slide a bolt into place. Not that it would do him much good.

I followed him upstairs and leaned hard against the door until, with a creak and a crunch, it flew open. By then his wife was making more noise than her children, who were still screaming from the next bedroom.

I went in, sat down on the edge of the bed and stared hard at the pair of them. They were sat straight up, blankets pulled up to their chins, arms around each other. Couldn't tell which one was shaking the most. I grinned at them and scratched at my itchy head. A worm dropped out of my hair and began to wriggle around on the coverlet.

'Might let you both live,' I told them. 'Might let your children live too. But you've got to do exactly what I say . . .'

'Don't hurt us, please,' begged the farmer. 'We'll do anything. Anything at all . . .'

I smiled. 'All you have to do is get Matthew Carter

to come here again. Make sure he arrives after dark, mind. Must be after dark – that's important. Round about midnight would be best. Just tell him another witch has been bothering you. And you need him here to sort her.'

'What if he won't come?' asked the trembling farmer, his eyes wide with fear.

'Well, in that case don't bother coming back. Because if you do, you'll find your family dead.'

He left before dawn, but I stayed close to the house and buried myself under a pile of straw in the barn until it was dark again. Just the tip of my bony nose was sticking out.

At dusk, that's where the child found me. The eldest daughter – no more than five years old, she was; plump little thing too. I could smell blood pumping through her warm body, and it took all my will power to let her live: I didn't want to have the mother in hysterics again. She had to be calm and peaceful when Matthew Carter arrived.

'When it goes dark,' said the child, 'my mother turns all the mirrors in the house to the wall.'

'Then she's a wise mother. That'll stop witches spying on you and your family.'

'But you're a witch and my mother says I should keep away from you,' said the child.

'Mothers know best,' I told her, 'so perhaps you should.'

'What's it like being a dead witch?'

'Itchy, child,' I told her, scratching at my head. 'Very itchy.'

'I could comb your hair if you like . . .' the child offered.

She ran off, and five minutes later came back with a comb. I had planned to kill her and the rest of her family eventually, but as she was combing the worms and insects out of my hair, I relented. I'd just kill the old farmer.

'Go back to your mother and tell her to take you and your sister as far away as possible from here,' I told her. 'And don't come back until well after dawn. Tell her to go right away. It's the only way to save your lives.'

I watched from the doorway of the barn as the mother took her children to safety, waddling like a duck as she set off on her little legs. Now I had to get myself ready. This time I would be the one waiting in ambush. Firstly I lit the entrance and the stairs well, using half a dozen candles.

A dead witch slowly loses her control of dark magic. But I hadn't been dead long and I had enough left for what was needed.

I heard the men approaching the front door. The old farmer had done well. I guessed that two would be planning to wait inside the house, like last time. I wasn't disappointed: luckily Matthew Carter was one of them. He came through the doorway first.

I smiled at him from the top of the stairs. 'Why don't we two have a little chat, Handsome Matthew?' I suggested pleasantly, giving him my sweetest smile. 'Just you and me alone together in the bedroom . . .'

As he started to climb the stairs towards me, his

tongue was hanging further out than a hungry dog's at the sight of fresh meat. Below, his companion looked very disappointed at not being invited into my company.

I was using the dark magic spells *glamour* and *fascination*, of course: the first could make even a dead witch appear extremely attractive; the second would have made him climb those stairs anyway.

'Come and sit next to me on the bed,' I bade the quisitor, closing the door behind us. 'Why don't we start with a little kiss?'

He did as I suggested, but just before his lips fastened on mine, the eager expression on his face turned to one of dismay. He'd smelled the real me: the stench of rot and decay, of dark damp loam and mouldy leaves. Then I uncloaked myself from the spell and his dismay turned to terror.

As I started to feed, that Matthew Carter screamed louder than the little pink pig I'd killed the previous night. I plunged my teeth deep into his neck and drained him with great hungry gulps. I felt the throb of his blood start to become erratic. Soon his heart stopped beating. Now he was Dead Matthew, and no longer of any interest to me.

I killed the second man in the doorway. The third and fourth were hiding in the barn, but I soon sniffed them out. There were others but they ran off in panic. Only the old farmer stayed. He thought his wife and children were still inside the house.

I'd had more blood than I needed and was full to bursting. Even so, I passed close to the old farmer as I walked across the yard – close enough to start his knees knocking.

'I've decided to let you live. But next time a witch begs at your gate,' I warned him, 'give her what she asks for.'

Then I was gone, heading back south towards Witch Dell.

There's something else I forgot to tell you. After I'd died I couldn't remember the name of the madwoman again. Strained my dead brain but it just wouldn't come. Now I'm a lot weaker and can't walk any more. Even a dead witch doesn't last for ever. And though my memories are slipping away fast, odd fragments keep coming back.

I can see that daft girl now as she's running past me on her way to knife the Fiend. And now I've remembered she was a Malkin and her name's on the tip of my tongue . . . the very tip. If only I could remember! I'd write it down then and our clan would seek her out for sure. She can't hide for ever. There are too many of us and she can't defeat us all.

It'll be light soon, so I've got to crawl back to the dell. Maybe I'll remember and write it down to-morrow night. That's if my fingers haven't dropped off. And if I can still remember the way here . . .

GRIMALKIN'S
TALE

My name is Grimalkin and I fear nobody. But my enemies fear me. With my scissors I snip the flesh of the dead; the clan enemies that I have slain in combat. I cut out their thumb-bones, which I wear around my neck as a warning to others. What else can I do? Without ruthlessness and savagery I would not survive even a week of the life I lead. I am the witch assassin of the Malkin clan.

Are you my enemy? Are you strong? Do you possess speed and agility? Have you had the training of a warrior? It matters nought to me. Run now! Run fast into the forest! I'll give you a few moments' start. An hour if you wish. Because no matter how hard you run, you'll never be fast enough, and before long I'll catch and kill you. I am a hunter and also a blacksmith skilled in the art of forging weapons. I could craft one especially for you; the steel that would surely take your life.

All the prey I hunt I will slay. If it is clothed in flesh, I will cut it. If it breathes, I will stop its breath. And your magic daunts me not, because I have magic of my own. And boggarts, ghosts and ghasts are no greater threat to me than they are to a spook. For I have looked into the darkness – into the greatest darkness of all – and I am no longer afraid.

My greatest enemy is the Fiend – the dark made flesh. Even as a child I disliked him; saw the way he controlled my clan; watched the way its coven fawned over him. That growing revulsion was something instinctive in me; a natural-born hatred. I knew that unless I did something, he would become a blight upon my life, a dark shadow over everything that I did.

But there is one way in which a witch can ensure

that he keeps his distance. A method that is very extreme but ensures that she is free of his fearsome power. She has to be close to him just once and bear his child. After he has inspected his offspring, he may not approach her again. Not unless she wishes it.

Most of the Fiend's children are abhumans – evil creatures that will do the bidding of the dark. Others grow to be powerful witches. But a few – and it is rare indeed – are born perfect human children untainted by evil. Mine was such a child.

I had never felt such love for another creature. To feel its warmth against my body, so trusting, so dependent, was wonderful beyond my dreams; something I had never imagined or anticipated. This little child loved me and I loved it in return; it depended upon me for life, and I was truly happy for the first time in my life. But such happiness rarely lasts.

I remember well the night that mine ended. The sun had just set and it was a warm summer's night, so I walked out into the garden to the rear of my cottage, cradling my child, humming to him softly to lull him to sleep. Suddenly lightning flashed overhead and I felt the ground move beneath my feet. The Fiend was about to appear and my heart lurched with fear. At the same time I was glad, because once he saw his son he would leave and never be able to visit me again. I would be rid of him for the rest of my life.

I was not prepared for the Fiend's reaction though. No sooner had he materialized than, with a roar of anger, he snatched my innocent baby boy and lifted him high in the air, ready to dash him to the ground.

'Please!' I begged. 'Don't hurt him. I'll do anything but please let him live . . .'

The Fiend never even looked at me. He was filled with wrath and cruelty. He smashed my child's fragile head against a rock. Then he vanished.

For a long time I was insane with grief. And then thoughts of revenge began to swirl within my head. Was it possible? Could I destroy the Fiend? Impossible or not, that became my goal and my only reason to continue living. I was still young – just turned seventeen – although strong and tall for my age. I had chosen to bear the Fiend's child as a means to be free of him for ever, and once I'd decided to pursue that course of action, nothing could stop me. Nothing would stop me now.

Wearing my thickest leather gloves, I forged three blades, each one tipped with silver alloy. It was painful for me even to be close to that metal which is harmful to all who have allegiance to the dark. But I gritted my teeth and did the work to the very best of my ability. Next I had to find my enemy – but that was the easy part.

The Fiend does not visit on every sabbath; some years he does not come at all. But Halloween was the most likely, and for some reason he particularly favours the Deanes at that time. So, shunning the Malkin celebration on Pendle Hill, I set off for Roughlee, the Deane village.

I arrived at dusk and settled myself down in a small wood overlooking the site of their sabbath fire. I was not too concerned about being detected. They would all be excited and distracted by their preparations, and besides, I had cloaked myself in my strongest magic, and such a thing as I planned would come as a surprise to them, to say the least. Most witches would consider it insane. The Deanes are not generally known for their imagination and are the least creative of the three clans.

Soon the witches began to gather and, combining their magic, they ignited the fire with a loud *whoosh*. Most of the fuel used was wood, but at its heart was a large pile of old bones, those no longer useful for dark magic. Most people call such a blaze a bonfire, but that name is derived from the word that witches use – *bone*-fire. The coven of the thirteen strongest witches formed a tight circle around its perimeter; their lesser sisters encircled them.

Just as the stink of the fire began to reach me, the Deanes began to curse their enemies. With wild shrieks and guttural cries, they called down death and destruction upon those they named. Someone old and enfeebled, or a witch grown careless might fall victim to such curses, but mostly they were wasting their time. All witches have defences against such dark magic. But I heard them name Caxton, the High Sheriff at Caster. He had arrested one of their number recently and now they wanted him dead. I knew that he would be lucky to survive the week.

As they finished cursing, there was a change in the fire: the yellow flames became orange, then red. It was the first sign that the Fiend was about to appear, and I heard an expectant gasp go up from the gathering. I stared towards the fire as he began to materialize. Able to make himself large or small, the Fiend was taking shape in all his fearsome majesty in order to impress his followers. The flames reached up to his knees, revealing that he was tall and broad – perhaps three times the size of an average man – with a long sinuous tail and the curved horns of a ram. His body was covered in thick black hair, and I saw the coven witches reach forward across the flames, eager to touch their dark lord.

I knew he would not stay for long. I had to strike now!

I left my hiding place in the trees and began to run as fast as I could, straight towards the fire. The witches would not see me approaching out of the darkness. Neither would they hear the pounding of my feet, distracted and excited as they were by the monster at the heart of the flames.

I had a blade in each hand; the third gripped tightly between my teeth. There was great danger here, but I hated the Fiend and was quite prepared to meet my death, either blasted by his power or torn to pieces by the Deanes. I cast my will before me; I had the power to keep him away but I did the reverse: I wished him to stay.

I ran through the gaps between those witches on the fringe of the gathering. As the throng became denser, I pushed them aside with my elbows and shoulders, and saw surprised and angry faces twisting towards me. At last I reached the coven and threw the first dagger. It struck the Fiend in the chest, burying itself up to the hilt. He shrieked long and loud. I'd hurt him badly and his cry of pain was music to my ears. But he twisted away in the flames so that my next two blades did not quite find their intended targets; even so, they buried themselves deep within his flesh.

For a moment he looked directly at me, his pupils red vertical slits. I had nothing with which to defend myself against the power that he could marshal: I waited to die. What was worse, however, he would, I well knew, find me after death and inflict never-ending torments on my soul.

Now I was willing him away. Would he go? Or would he destroy me first?

To my relief, he simply vanished, taking the flames of the fire with him so that we were all plunged into darkness. The rule had held. I had carried his child, so he could not be in my presence; not unless I wished it.

There was confusion all around me, shrieks of anger and fear; witches running in all directions. I slipped away into the darkness and made my escape. Of course, I knew that they would send assassins after me. It meant I'd have to kill or be killed.

I ran, heading north and passing beyond Pendle Hill, then curved away west towards the distant sea. I knew exactly where I was going, having planned my escape far in advance. On the flatlands, east of the river Wyre's estuary, was the spot where I would make my stand. I had wrapped myself in a cloak of dark magic, but it would not be strong enough to hide me from all those who followed me. I needed to fight in a place where I might gain an advantage.

There is a line of three villages there: Hambleton, Staumin and Preesall, aligned roughly north to south, joined by a narrow track that sometimes becomes impassable because of the tide. On all sides they are surrounded by soggy moss. The river is tidal, with extensive salt marshes, and north-west of Staumin, right on the sea margin, is Arm Hill, a small mound of firm ground that rises above the grassy tussocks and treacherous channels along which the tide races to trap the unwary. On one side is the river; on the other, the marsh, and nobody can cross it without being seen from that vantage point.

I waited for my pursuers, knowing there would be more than one. My crime against the Deane clan was terrible indeed. If they caught me, I would die slowly and in great pain. The first of my enemies came into sight at dusk, picking her way slowly across the marsh grass.

As a witch, I have many skills and talents. One of these proved very useful now. As an enemy approaches, I instantly know her worth: her strength and ability in combat. The one crossing the marsh towards me now was competent enough, but not of the first order. No doubt her talents as a tracker and her power to penetrate my dark magical cloak had brought this witch to me first.

I waited until she was close, then showed myself to her. I was standing on that small hill, clearly outlined against the fading red of the western sky. She ran towards me, a blade in each hand. She did not weave; made no attempt to make herself a difficult target.

It was me or her. One of us would die. So be it!

I pulled my favourite throwing knife from my belt.

This one was not tipped with silver alloy but that wasn't necessary; it was sufficient to slay a witch. I hurled it at my attacker and it took her in the throat. She made a little gurgling noise, dropped to her knees and fell face down in the marsh grass.

She was the first human being I had ever killed, and I felt a momentary pang. But it quickly passed as I concentrated on ensuring my own survival. I hid the witch's body under a shelf of grass tussocks, pushing her down into the mud. I did not take her heart. We had faced each other in honourable combat and she had lost. One night that witch would return from the dead, crawling across the marsh in search of prey. As she was no further threat to me, I would not deny her that.

I waited almost three days for the next to find me. There were two and they arrived together. We fought at noon, the late autumn sun painting the slow tidal ebb of the river blood-red. I was strong and fast, but they were veterans of such fights, with a repertoire of tricks that I had never encountered. They hurt me

badly, and the scars of those wounds mark my body to this day. The struggle lasted over an hour, and it was close, but at last victory was mine, and the bodies of two more Deanes went into the marsh.

It was almost three weeks before I was fit to travel, but in that time they sent no more avengers after me. The trail had gone cold and it was unlikely that anyone would have recognized me that night when I attacked the Fiend. I thought long and hard about what had happened. I had hurt the Devil. Would he try to kill me in some way? Or might I find a way to destroy him first?

I consulted a scryer. Her name was Martha Ribstalk, an incomer from the far north. She did not use a mirror to see the future; her method was to peer into a steaming blood-tainted cauldron, one boiling up thumb- and finger-bones to strip away the dead flesh. At that time, before the rise of Mab, the young scryer of the Mouldheels, she was the foremost practitioner of that dark art. I visited her one hour after midnight, as we had arranged. One hour after she had drunk the blood of an enemy and performed the necessary rituals.

'Do you accept my money?' I demanded.

She nodded, so I tossed three coins into the cauldron.

'Be seated!' she commanded sternly, pointing to the cold stone flags before the large bubbling pot. The air was tainted with blood, and each breath I took increased the metallic taste at the back of my tongue.

I obeyed, sitting cross-legged and gazing up at her through the steam. She had remained standing so that she was higher than me, a tactic often practised by those who wish to dominate others. But I was not cowed and met her gaze calmly.

'What did you see?' I demanded. 'What is my future?'

She did not speak for a long time. It pleased her to keep me waiting. I think Ribstalk was annoyed because I had asked a question rather than waiting to be told the outcome of her scrying.

'You have chosen an enemy,' she said at last. 'The

most powerful enemy any mortal could face. The outcome should be simple. Unless you wish it, the Fiend cannot approach you, but he will await your death, then seize your soul and subject it to everlasting torments. But there is something else; something that I cannot see clearly. An uncertainty . . . another force that may intervene. Just a glimmer of hope for you . . .'

She paused, then stepped closer and peered into the steam. Once again there was a long pause. 'There is someone there . . . a child just born—'

'Who is this child?' I demanded.

'I cannot see him clearly,' Martha Ribstalk admitted. 'Someone hides him from my sight. And as for you, even with his intervention, only one highly skilled with weapons could hope to survive. Only one with the speed and ruthlessness of a witch assassin. Only the greatest of all assassins – more deadly even than Kernolde – could do that. Nothing less will do. So what hope have you?' she mocked.

Kernolde was then the assassin of the Malkins. A fearsome woman of great strength and speed, who had slain twenty-seven challengers for her position – three each year, as this was the tenth year of her reign.

I rose to my feet and smiled down at Ribstalk. 'I will slay Kernolde and then take her place. I will become the witch assassin of the Malkins – the greatest of them all.'

I turned and walked away, listening to the scryer cackling with mocking laughter behind me. But mine were not vain boasts. I believed that I could do it. I truly believed.

Three pretenders to the position of Malkin assassin were trained annually, but this year one place remained to be filled. No wonder – for most believed it was certain death to face Kernolde. The other two witches had been in training for six months. Thus half a year remained before the three days assigned for the challenges. That was the time left for me to gain some of the skills necessary. Barely time for most to learn the rudiments of the assassin's trade.

The training school was in a clearing in Crow Wood.

My first day there filled me with dismay. The other two trainees had no confidence, and death was already written on their foreheads. I grew more and more disgruntled with every hour that passed.

At last, just before dark, I spoke my mind. We three were sitting cross-legged on the ground, looking up at Grist Malkin, our trainer. He was droning on about blade-fighting. Behind him were two sour-faced matriarchs of our clan, both witches. They were there to ensure we did not use magic against our trainer.

'You are a fool, Grist!' I snapped, no longer able to control my irritation. 'You've already prepared twenty-seven defeated challengers before us. What can you teach us but how to lose and how to die?'

For a long time he did not speak but simply locked eyes with me and glared, his face twitching with fury. He was a big man, a head taller than me and heavily muscled. But I was not afraid and met his gaze calmly. It was he who looked away first.

'On your feet, girl!' he commanded.

I stood slowly and smiled.

'Take that grin off your face. Don't look at me!' he barked. 'Look straight ahead. Have some respect for your teacher. Listening to me might just save your life . . .'

He began to circle me slowly. I watched him out of the corner of my eye as he disappeared behind my left shoulder. Suddenly he seized me in a bear hug, trying to squeeze the breath from my body. I felt a sharp pain as one of my ribs cracked.

'Let that be a lesson to you!' he cried, throwing me down into the dirt.

But I made sure that he did not speak again: I was on my feet in an instant and broke his nose with my left fist, the punch knocking him to the ground.

The struggle between us was over quickly. I did not let him get close to me again. My blows were swift and executed with precision. Within moments one of his eyes was swollen and closed. Seconds later, his forehead was split open and blood was running into his other eye. Unable to see, he could offer little defence and I quickly administered a chop, bringing him to his knees.

The two crones knelt at Grist's side. One was his mother, and I saw that tears were streaming down her cheeks.

'I could kill you now,' I cried, 'but you're just a man and hardly worth the trouble!'

I began to walk away, but before I entered the trees I turned. I had one last thing to say.

'I'm leaving this place,' I told them. 'But I'll return to face Kernolde.'

There is one thing that I have not yet told you. Grist had trained my older sister, Wrekinda. She was Kernolde's fifth victim: one more reason to kill the witch assassin.

It was fortunate that I was already skilled in the ways of the forest and crafting weapons. Fortunate too that, as the third accepted for training, I'd be the last to face Kernolde. Even in defeat the other challengers might weaken her, or at least drain some of her strength.

So I trained myself. I worked hard; invited danger; ate well; built up my strength; swam daily to increase my endurance for combat – mile upon mile despite the winter cold. I also crafted the best blades of which I was capable and carried them in sheaths about my body, which grew stronger and faster by the day. I ran up and down the steep slopes of Pendle to improve my stamina, readying myself for the fight to the death against Kernolde.

In a forest far to the north, beyond the boundaries of the County, I faced a pack of howling wolves. They circled me, moving ever closer, death glittering in their hungry eyes. I held a throwing knife in each hand. The first wolf leaped for my throat; leaped and died as my blade found its throat first. The second died too. Next I drew my long blade, awaiting the third attack. With one powerful stroke I struck the animal's head from its body. Before the pack turned and fled my wrath, seven lay dead, their blood staining the white snow red.

At last the time to face Kernolde arrived and I returned to Pendle. Did I say I hoped the other challengers would weaken the witch assassin? My hopes were short-lived. She slew each with ease; both were dead in less than an hour. On the third night it was my turn.

The challenge always takes place north of the Devil's Triangle, where the villages of the Malkins, Deanes and Mouldheels are located. Kernolde chose as her killing ground Witch Dell, where witches are taken by their families after death; taken there and buried amongst the trees to rise with the full moon, scratching their way back to the surface to feed upon small animals and unwary human intruders. Some of the dead witches are strong and can roam for miles seeking their prey. Kernolde used these dead things as her allies – sometimes as her eyes, nose and ears; sometimes as weapons. More than one challenger had been drained of blood by the dead before Kernolde took her thumb-bones as proof of victory. But she often triumphed without these allies. She was skilled with blades, ropes, traps and pits full of spikes; once her opponents were captured or incapacitated, she would often simply strangle them to death.

All this I knew before my challenge started; I had thought long and hard about it and had visited this dell many times during the previous months. I had gone there in daylight, when the dead witches were dormant and Kernolde was out hunting prey in distant parts of the County. I had sniffed out every inch of the wood; knew every tree, the whereabouts of every pit and trap.

So I was ready. I stood outside the dell in the shadow of the trees just before midnight, the appointed time for combat to begin. High to my left was the large brooding mass of Pendle, its eastern slopes bathed in the light of the full moon, which was high in the sky to the south. Within moments a beacon flared at the summit, sparks shooting upwards into the air, signalling that the witching hour had begun.

Immediately I did what no other challenger had done before. Most crept into the dell, nervous and fearful, in dread of what they faced. Some were braver but still entered cautiously. I was different. I announced my presence in a loud, clear voice.

'I'm here, Kernolde! My name is Grimalkin and I am your death!' I shouted into the dell. 'I'm coming for *you*, Kernolde! I'm coming for *you*! And nothing living or dead can stop me!'

It was not just bravado, although that played a part. It was the product of much thought and calculation. I knew that my shouts would summon up the dead witches, and that's what I wanted. Now I would know where they were.

You see, most dead witches are slow and I could outrun them. It was the powerful ones I had to beware of. One of them was named Grim Gertrude because of her intimidating appearance, and she was both strong and relatively speedy for one who had been dead more than a century. She roamed far and wide beyond the dell, hunting for blood. But tonight she would be waiting there: she was Kernolde's closest accomplice, well-rewarded in blood, for she helped to bring about each victory.

I waited for about fifteen minutes – long enough to let the slowest witch get near. I'd already sniffed out Gertrude, the old one. She'd been close to the edge of the dell for some time but had chosen not to venture out into the open: she had retreated deeper into the trees so that her slower sisters could attack me first. I heard the rustling of leaves and the occasional faint crack of a twig as they shuffled forward. They were slow, but I didn't underestimate them. Dead witches have great strength, and once they fasten onto your flesh, they cannot be easily prised free. Soon they begin to suck your blood until you weaken and can fight no more. Some of them would be on the ground, hiding within the dead leaves, ready to reach out and grasp at my ankles as I sped by.

I sprinted into the trees. I had already sniffed out Kernolde. She was where I expected, waiting beneath the branches of the oldest oak in the dell. That was her tree; the one in which she stored her magic; her place of power.

A hand reached up towards me from the leaves.

Without breaking my stride, I unsheathed a dagger from the scabbard on my left thigh and pinned the dead witch to a thick, gnarled tree root. I thrust the blade into her wrist rather than her palm, making it more difficult for her to tear herself free.

The next witch shuffled towards me from my right, her face lit by a shaft of moonlight. Saliva was dribbling down her chain and onto her tattered gown, which was covered in dark stains. She jabbered curses at me, eager for my blood. Instead she got my blade, which I plucked from my right shoulder sheath, hurling it towards her. The point took her in the throat, throwing her backwards. I ran on even faster.

Four more times my blades sliced into dead flesh, and by now most of the other witches were left behind – the slow and those maimed by my blades. But Kernolde and the powerful old one waited somewhere ahead. I wore eight sheaths that day; each contained a blade. Now only two remained.

I leaped a hidden pit, then a second. Even though

they were covered with leaves and mud, I knew they were there. At last the old one barred my path. I came to a halt and prepared myself to attack her. Let her come to me!

I looked at Grim Gertrude, noting the tangled hair that came down to her knees. She was grim indeed and well-named! Maggots and beetles scuttled within the rank curtain that obscured all of her face save one malevolent eye and an elongated tooth jutting upwards over her top lip almost as far as her left nostril.

She rushed towards me, kicking up leaves, her hands extended to rend my face or squeeze my throat. She was fast for a dead witch; very fast. But not fast enough.

With my left hand I drew the largest of my blades from its scabbard at my hip. This was not crafted for throwing; it was more like a short sword, with two razor-sharp edges. I leaped forward and cut Grim Gertrude's head clean from her shoulders. It bounced on a root and rolled away. I ran on, glancing back to see her hands searching amongst the pile of rotting leaves where it had come to rest.

Now for Kernolde. She was waiting beneath her tree. I saw that ropes hung from the branches, ready to bind and hang my body. She was rubbing her back against the bark, drawing strength for the fight. But I was not afraid – she looked more like an old bear ridding itself of fleas than the dreaded witch assassin feared by all. Running directly towards her at full tilt, I drew the last of my throwing knives and hurled it straight at her throat. End over end it spun, my aim fast and true, but she knocked it aside with a disdainful flick of her wrist. Undaunted, I increased my pace and prepared to use the long blade. But then the ground opened up beneath my feet: my heart lurched and I fell into a hidden pit.

The moon was high, and as I fell I saw the sharp spikes below waiting to impale me. I twisted desperately, trying to protect my body, but to avoid every spike was impossible. All I could do was contort myself so that only one spike speared into me, inflicting the least damage.

The least, did I say? It hurt me enough: the spike pierced right through my thigh. Down its length I slid until I hit the ground hard and all the breath left my body, the long blade flying from my hand to lie out of reach.

I lay there, trying to breathe and control the pain in my leg. The spikes were sharp, thin and very long – more than six feet – so there was no way I could lift my leg and free it. I cursed my folly. I had thought myself safe, but Kernolde had dug another pit – probably the previous night. No doubt she'd been aware of my forays into the dell and had waited until the last moment to add another trap.

A witch assassin must constantly adapt and learn from her own mistakes. Even as I lay there, facing my imminent death, I recognized my stupidity. I had been too confident and had underestimated Kernolde. If I survived, I swore to temper my attitude with a smidgeon of caution. *If* . . .

The witch assassin's broad moon-face appeared above and she looked down at me without uttering a word. I was fast and I excelled with blades. I was strong too – but not as strong as Kernolde. Not for nothing did some call her Kernolde the Strangler. Once victorious, Kernolde sometimes hung her victims by their thumbs before slowly asphyxiating them. Not this time though. She had seen what I had achieved already and would take no chances. She would soon put her hands about my throat and squeeze the breath and life from my body. I knew that I would die here.

She began to climb down into the pit. I was calm and ready to die if need be, but I had already thought of something. I had a slim chance of survival.

As Kernolde reached the bottom of the pit and began to weave her way towards me through the spikes, flexing her big muscular hands, I prepared myself to cope with pain. Not the pain she would inflict upon me; that which I chose myself.

My hands were strong; my arms and shoulders

capable of exerting extreme leverage. The spikes in the pit were thin but sturdy; flexible, not brittle. But I had to try. From where I lay I could reach only the one that had pierced my leg, so I seized it and began to bend it. Back and forth, back and forth, I flexed and twisted the spike, each movement sending pain shooting down my leg and up into my body. But I gritted my teeth and worked away at the spike, until it finally yielded and broke, coming away in my hands.

Quickly I lifted my leg clear of the stump and knelt to face Kernolde, my blood running down to soak the earthen floor of the killing pit. I held the spike like a spear and pointed it towards her. Before her hands could reach my throat I would pierce her heart.

But the witch assassin had drawn much of her stored magic out of the tree, and now she halted and concentrated, beginning to hurl shards of darkness towards me. First of all she tried *dread* – that dark spell a witch uses to terrify her enemies, holding them in thrall to fear. Terror tried to claim me and my teeth began to chitter-chatter like those of the dead on the Halloween sabbath.

Kernolde's magic was strong; but not strong enough. I braced myself and shrugged aside her spell. Soon its effects receded and it bothered me no more than the cold wind that had blown down from the arctic ice when I slew the wolves and left their bodies on the snow.

Next she used the unquiet dead – the 'bone-bound' – against me, hurling towards me the spirits she had trapped in Limbo. They clung to my body, dragging my arm down so that it took all my strength to keep hold of that spike. They were strong and fortified by dark magic – one was a strangler, who gripped my throat so hard that Kernolde herself might have been squeezing it. The worst of them was an ab-human spirit, the ghost of one born of the Fiend and a witch. He darkened my eyes and thrust his long cold fingers into my ears so that I thought my head was about to burst, but I fought back and cried out into the darkness and silence:

'I'm still here, Kernolde! Still to be reckoned with. I am Grimalkin, your doom!'

My eyes cleared and the abhuman's fingers left my ears with a *pop* so that sound rushed back. The weight was gone from my arms and I struggled to my feet, taking aim with the spike. Kernolde rushed at me then – a big ugly bear of a woman with strangler's hands. But my aim was true. I thrust the spear right into her heart and she fell at my feet, her blood soaking into the earth to mix with mine. She was choking, trying to speak, so I bent and put my ear close to her lips.

'You're just a girl,' she croaked. 'To be defeated by a girl, after all this time . . . How can this be?'

'Your time is over and mine is just beginning,' I told her. 'This girl took your life and now she will take your bones.'

After taking what I needed, I lifted Kernolde's body out of the pit using her own ropes. Finally I hung her up by her feet so that at dawn the birds could peck her bones clean. That done, I passed through the dell without incident: the dead witches kept their distance.

Grim Gertrude was on her hands and knees, still rooting around in the mouldy leaves, trying to find her head. Without eyes it would prove difficult.

When I emerged from the trees, the clan was waiting to greet me. I held up Kernolde's thumb-bones, and they bowed their heads in acknowledgement of what I'd done; even Katrise, the head of the coven of thirteen, made obeisance. When they looked up, I saw the new respect in their eyes; the fear too.

Now I would begin my quest to destroy my enemy, the Fiend. The spikes in the pit had given me an idea. What if I crafted a sharp spike of silver alloy and somehow impaled the Fiend on it? What if it went right through his heart? And if that didn't work, there had to be some other way . . .

One day I *will* find a way to destroy him.

My name is Grimalkin. I am the witch assassin of the Malkins and I fear nobody.

ALICE AND THE BRAIN GUZZLER

CHAPTER 1
MY NAME IS ALICE DEANE

My name is Alice Deane and I was born into the Pendle witch clans. Didn't want to be a witch, did I? But sometimes you've no choice and things just happen.

I remember the night my aunt, Bony Lizzie, came for me. Like to think I was upset, but I don't remember crying. My mam and dad had been cold and dead in the damp earth for three days and I still hadn't managed to shed a single tear – though it wasn't for want of trying. Tried to remember the good times, I really did. And there were a few, despite the fact that they fought like cat and dog and clouted me even harder than they hit each other. I mean, you should be

117

upset, shouldn't you? It's your own mam and dad and they've just died so you *should* be able to squeeze out one tear at least.

I was staying with my other aunt, Agnes Sowerbutts. She'd taken me in and wanted to bring me up proper and give me a good start in life. Fat chance of that!

The day had been a scorcher and there was a bad summer storm that night – forks of devil-lightning sizzling across the sky and crashes of thunder shaking the walls of the cottage and rattling the pots and pans. But that was nowt compared to what Lizzie did. There was a hammering at the door fit to wake the rotting dead, and when Agnes drew back the bolt, Bony Lizzie strode into the room, her black hair matted with rain, water streaming from her cape to cascade onto the stone flags. Agnes was scared but she stood her ground, placing herself between me and Lizzie.

'Leave the girl alone!' she said calmly, trying to be brave. 'Her home is with me now. She'll be well looked after, don't you worry.'

JOSEPH DELANEY

Lizzie's first response was a sneer. They say there's a family resemblance and that I'm the spitting image of her. But I could never have twisted my face the way she did that night. It was enough to turn the milk sour or send the cat shrieking up the chimney as if Old Nick himself was reaching for its tail.

'The girl belongs to me, Sowerbutts,' Lizzie said, her voice cold and quiet, filled with malice. 'We share the same dark blood. I can teach her what she has to know. I'm the one she needs.'

'Alice needn't be a witch like you!' Agnes retorted. 'Her mam and dad weren't witches, so why should she follow your dark path? Leave her be. Leave the girl with me and get about your business.'

'She's the blood of a witch inside her and that's enough!' Lizzie hissed angrily. 'You're just an outsider and not fit to raise the girl.'

It wasn't true. Agnes was a Deane all right, but she'd married a good man from Whalley, an ironmonger. When he died, she'd returned to Roughlee, where the Deane witch clan made its home.

'I'm her aunt and I'll be a mother to her now,' Agnes retorted. She still spoke bravely but her face was pale, and now I could see her plump chin wobbling, her hands fluttering and trembling with fear.

Next thing, Lizzie stamped her left foot. It was as easy as that. In the twinkling of an eye, the fire died in the grate, the candles flickered and went out, and the whole room became instantly dark, cold and terrifying. I heard Agnes scream with fear; I was screaming myself and desperate to get out. I would have run through the door, jumped through a window or even scrabbled my way up the chimney – I'd have done anything, just to escape.

I did get out, but with Lizzie at my side. She just seized me by the wrist and dragged me off into the night. It was no use trying to resist. She was too strong and she held me tight, her nails digging into my skin. I belonged to her now and there was no way she was ever going to let me go. And that night she began my training as a witch. It was the start of all my troubles.

* * *

That first night in her cottage was the worst. Lizzie started off by showing me the crone she used as her servant. The old woman was standing outside the front door, leaning back against the window ledge, and didn't look too friendly.

She was old all right, but big and ugly too, with long grey hair hanging almost to her waist. She wore a dirty smock, but her short sleeves showed big, muscly, hairy arms that could easily have belonged to a man. Didn't like the look of her one bit. She just stared at me – didn't say a word.

'Her name is Nanna Nuckle and she's a very useful servant,' Lizzie told me. 'Only problem is, she can't go outside in daylight. So she sleeps then. Good at lifting big iron pots and at keeping disobedient girls in check, though. Best do as you're told, girl. She'll be watching you.'

Soon as we got inside, she locked me in a room without a window. Ain't many times in my life I've been as scared as that. It was so dark I couldn't see my hands in front of my face. Didn't smell good either. Something had died in there recently. Not sure if it was animal or human – maybe something in between. But it had breathed its last, slowly and in great pain. Didn't take much sniffing to work that out.

Sniffing is a gift. Born that way, I was. Always been able to do it. But I didn't know then that you could be trained so that it would become a powerful sense, almost as useful as the eyes in your head. That was the first lesson Lizzie gave me. Dragged me out of that stinky dark room well before dawn and took me outside. There were three small fires burning, and above each, a black bubbling iron pot with a wooden lid.

'Well, girl,' Lizzie said, that sneer on her face again, 'let's see how strong your gift is. In one of those pots is your breakfast. Find it and you'll eat well. Lift the wrong lid and you'll eat what's inside anyway. Either that or it'll eat you!'

After the storm the air was much cooler and, shivering with cold and fear, I stared at the three pots for a long time, watching the lids twitch and jerk as the water bubbled and the steam rose. At last Lizzie lost patience and gripped my shoulder hard, pushing me close to the pot on the left.

'Get on with it, girl, if you know what's good for you!'

I was scared of Lizzie and she was hurting my shoulder, her sharp nails pressing right into the flesh as if searching for my bones, so I did what she said. I sniffed three times.

Didn't smell good. Something wick in there, I felt sure; something alive when it ought to be dead; something thin and twiggy but still moving in that bubbly, boiling water.

Lizzie dragged me along to face the centre pot. Sniffed three times again and didn't like what was inside that one either. Something soft and squishy, it was. Something that once grew in the ground – but not fit to eat, I was sure of that. One bite of what was inside would boil your blood, make your eyes swell and pop right out of your head. Didn't want to eat that any more than what was in the first pot.

The third pot contained rabbit – tender, delicious pieces of it melting off the bone and almost ready to eat. One sniff and I knew that for sure.

'This one,' I said. 'I'll eat rabbit for breakfast.' I lifted the lid to prove that I was right.

'That was easy enough, girl, but you're right – this morning you'll enjoy your breakfast,' Lizzie said. 'Now, let's see what's in the middle pot. What do you think it is?'

'Something poisonous. Just one mouthful and you'd be dead.'

'But what kind of poison?' demanded Lizzie. 'Can you tell me the ingredients?'

I shook my head and sniffed again. 'Maybe toadstools . . . not sure.'

'Lift the lid and take a look!'

I replaced the lid on my breakfast and lifted the one over the centre pot. Stepped back right away, I did. Didn't want to breathe in that poisonous steam. There were pieces of toadstool churning in the boiling water.

'Nine different toadstools in there,' Lizzie told me. 'By the end of the month, with just three sniffs you'll know every one by name. You've a lot of work ahead of you, girl, but the gift is strong inside you. Just needs developing, that's all. Now try the third lid . . .'

This pot really scared me. What lay within? What could survive in that boiling water? As I hesitated, Lizzie dug her nails deeper into my shoulder, hurting me so much that, despite my fear, I reached for the lid.

As I slowly lifted it, Lizzie released me and stepped back. I got the shock of my life. Almost wet myself, I did. A small evil-looking face was watching me from within the pot. The head of the creature was just above the boiling water but I couldn't see its body. Suddenly it leaped straight at my face. I dropped the lid and ducked.

It went straight over my head. I turned and saw that it had landed high on Lizzie's chest, its ugly head nestling at her throat. It convulsed and burrowed down into her dress, hiding.

'This is Old Spig, my familiar,' Lizzie said with a fond smile. 'He's my eyes, nose and ears. Doesn't miss much, does Old Spig. So you do as you're told, girl, or he'll find you out. And once he tells me, you'll be in real trouble. Then I'll teach you all about pain . . .'

That was my first sight of Lizzie's familiar. Mostly she was a witch who used bone-magic, but for Lizzie, Old Spig was well worth his keep. He was scary, and from that first time I set eyes on him I knew he'd give me trouble.

After tucking into that delicious rabbit I felt a bit better. And for the rest of that day all I had to do was a few household chores; it wasn't so different to what I'd been doing while staying with Agnes. I had to lay the cooking fire, wash the pots, pans and cutlery, and prepare a lamb stew for our evening meal. Nanna Nuckle didn't help; she stayed in her room all day because she couldn't stand daylight. She wasn't a witch, so I couldn't understand why this was. But when I asked Lizzie, she just told me to mind my own business.

Didn't do much cleaning though, except in my own room. It seemed that Lizzie liked the cottage to be dirty. Made her feel comfortable. There was one room I wasn't allowed inside – I reckoned it was the one where Old Spig spent most of his time, and I didn't like the sounds that were coming out of there. Couldn't hear Spig, but something was whining like it was in pain, so I kept well clear.

But, looking on the bright side, I'd survived Lizzie's first test. Old Spig scared me rotten, but apart from him, maybe living with Lizzie wouldn't be quite as bad as I'd expected.

'Are you brave, girl?' Lizzie asked me once I'd finished my work. 'A witch needs to be brave! I've got something in mind that only a really brave girl can cope with.'

I nodded at Bony Lizzie. I didn't want to admit that I was scared, but my teeth were chattering with fear, and she smiled at my discomfort as if it gave her

pleasure. The sun had been down about half an hour
and we were standing in her small front room, which
was very gloomy. A single candle made from black
wax was flickering on the mantelpiece, filling the
corners with strange shadows.

'Are you strong, girl?'

'Strong for my age,' I told her, nodding again, my
voice quavering.

'Well, all you have to do is go down into Witch Dell
and bring me back a special jug. You'll find it buried
close to the trunk of the tallest oak there. Dig where the
moon casts the tree's shadow at midnight!'

My whole body began to shake then. The dell was
full of dead witches. They came out at night, looking
for blood.

'Are you going to be a witch, girl?' Lizzie asked. 'Is
that what you want?'

I didn't really want to become a witch, but to say no
would have made Lizzie really angry, so I nodded for
the third time.

'Then don't be afeard of dead witches. Besides, those

down in the dell won't do you much harm. They're all sisters-in-death. They don't bother each other much and they won't bother you. Get ye gone but be sure to be back afore dawn. What's in the jug will spoil in daylight!'

CHAPTER 2
A WITCH YOU'LL ALWAYS BE

Witch Dell was north of the Devil's Triangle, the three villages where the Malkins, Deanes and Mouldheels made their homes. It was a clear night, the moon waxing to three quarters full. Pendle Hill to the west was bathed in silver light, and so bright was that moonshine that only two stars in the sky were visible.

When I reached the dell, it was less than half an hour before midnight so I couldn't afford to dawdle and walked straight in. It was gloomy, a patchwork of dappled moon-shadows, the gnarled roots like ogres' fingers clutching the ground. But last year's autumn leaves were heaped thickly around the trunks of *some* of the trees. That bothered me. They could have been blown there by the wind, but a dark alternative wormed its way into my head.

They could have been piled there by dead witches, couldn't they? Dank loamy beds to rest dead bones under on a chill night; leafy lairs from which to strike, grasping the ankles of unwary travellers before dragging them down for a blood-feast.

Had to trust what Lizzie had told me though – that they wouldn't hurt me; that the dead forgot clan enmities. But I'd not gone more than a hundred yards when I heard something heading my way, feet shuffling through the leaves. Something nasty was approaching . . .

So I sniffed her out. It was a dead witch all right, but there was something odd about her. It was only when she stepped into a shaft of moonlight that I saw that she didn't have a head. She was carrying it under her arm like a big pumpkin. So I knew who she was right away!

It was Grim Gertrude, the oldest witch in the dell.

Years earlier, the witch assassin Grimalkin had sliced off her head. Best thing to do in the circumstances. That had slowed her down all right! Story goes that it was almost a month before she finally found it again. So she wasn't going to let it go now. Gripping it really tightly, she was.

Gertrude turned so that she was facing me, her eyes watching me. The glassy, rheumy eyes glistened in the moonlight and the pale lips moved, but no sound reached my ears. The head wasn't connected to the neck so her voice-box didn't work. But I could read her lips and knew what she was saying:

'Who are you? What clan are ye from? Speak while you've still breath in your scrawny body!'

'My name's Alice Deane, but my mother was a Malkin.'

'As you're half Malkin, I'll let you live, but you're not welcome here, child,' mouthed the lips. 'The living don't come here – not if they know what's good for them!'

I began to tremble. Lizzie had lied to me. She'd not

133

wanted to risk coming to the dell herself after dark so she'd sent me to risk my neck.

'Bony Lizzie sent me to get something, she did. It's a jug buried near the biggest oak in the dell . . .'

Gertrude stepped nearer to me and suddenly reached out to grab me by the arm. She pulled me close, and a damp, loamy, rotting smell filled my nostrils, making me want to retch.

'*Do you do everything that Lizzie tells you?*' she asked.

'She's my mistress and is training me to be a witch. Don't have much choice, do I?'

Gertrude sniffed me three times. '*You were born a witch and a witch you'll always be. Don't have to be Lizzie who trains you. You've got the makings of somebody really strong. You could find someone else to show you the way.*'

'Only been with Lizzie just over a day,' I told her. 'Might give her till the end of the week. Let's see how she shapes up.'

Couldn't lip-read what Gertrude said next. It

took me a few moments to realize that she was laughing.

'*You've got spirit, girl,*' her lips mouthed at last. '*If Lizzie don't suit, I can teach you all about the dark. Won't be the first dead witch who's trained a young girl and shown her what's proper. Can't do dark magic myself – been dead too long for that – but I do still remember how things are done, and I can see that the power's in you. Together, we could bring it out. We'd make a good team, me and you. Help each other. So think it over, girl. You know where to find me. Now go and get what Lizzie needs. I won't stand in your way.*'

I watched the dead witch shuffle off into the trees, her head still tucked underneath her arm. Dead and smelly, she was, but still nicer than Lizzie.

I went on till I reached the tallest oak tree in the dell, waited until exactly midnight, and then dug with my fingers close to the trunk in the shadow cast by the moon. Didn't take me long to find what Lizzie wanted because it wasn't buried very deep. It was a small earthen jug. The lid was fastened on tight so I didn't try to force it off. It was Lizzie's business anyway. So I took it back to her.

'Well done, girl!' she said, giving me a twisted smile. 'Now get yourself to bed. I've got work to do and it's not something you're ready to see yet. You'll need months of training afore you're ready for that.'

So I went up to my room and tried to sleep. It took me a long while because every time I closed my eyes I kept seeing scary Gertrude. The noises coming from downstairs didn't help either. I heard what sounded like a wild animal growling and then, a little later, a young child bawling its eyes out. When I finally nodded off, I slept for hours. Lizzie didn't bother to wake me and I didn't get up till late afternoon.

'Look what the cat's dragged in!' Lizzie said as I staggered downstairs. 'Now you're up at last you'd best get busy making supper. Fancy a good beef stew, I do. I'm going out and won't be back until after dark. Make sure that stew's waiting for me and that it's piping hot.'

Sleeping in late had given me a headache so I went for a stroll first to clear my head. Enjoyed my walk and got back later than I'd intended, so I had to rush a bit with the meal. The sun had set before I even got started. I chopped up onions, potatoes, carrots and beets, and added them to the big iron pot, where chunks of beef were already boiling away over the kitchen fire. Only really good at cooking one meal, I am – that's rabbit turned on a spit over an open fire – but though I say it myself, about half an hour later, when I took a sip from the ladle, that stew was quite tasty.

All I needed to do now was put the lid on and let it simmer till Lizzie got back. Had to root through her mucky cupboards and it took me quite a while to find the lid. While I was giving it a good scrubbing in the sink, I heard a noise behind me – what sounded like a splash. I turned round but could see nothing. Puzzled, I dried the lid, then carried it across to the pot.

What I saw next made me come to a sudden halt

137

and drop the lid, which fell onto the flags with a loud clang. Two eyes were staring at me from the pot. It was Lizzie's familiar, Old Spig – but only his ugly head was visible; the rest of him was hidden by the bubbling stew. His mouth was wide open and he was slurping up the boiling liquid just as fast as he could.

'That's Lizzie's supper! She ain't going to thank you for eating it!' I warned him.

Spig's eyes widened a little but he didn't bother to reply. He just kept on gulping down the stew as if he couldn't get enough of it.

I started to get angry. Soon there wouldn't be enough left for our suppers and Lizzie would be really annoyed with me, to say the least. Not that I fancied the stew much now that Spig had decided to swim in it.

'Get out of there, you dirty little thing!' I snapped.

Old Spig's head rose out of the stew so that I could just see the beginning of his narrow scaly neck. '*What* did you just call me?' he demanded.

His voice was harsh and surprisingly deep for such a small creature. There was something so malevolent about it that made the hairs on the back of my neck stand up.

'Called you a dirty little thing!' I said. 'It ain't nice, you crawling around in our supper like that. Lizzie won't like it. I'll tell her what you've done unless you get out of my pot right away.'

He leaped out towards me and I stepped back quickly. But he hadn't meant to jump on me. He fell short of where I'd been standing and perched on the edge of the mantelpiece. He was covered in soupy stew and it started to ooze from his body and form a puddle underneath him. Despite that, I was now able to get a proper look at him for the first time.

Old Spig was about the size of a small rabbit but he was almost all head – and an uglier one I'd never seen. It was covered with green scales, apart from the face. He had a hooked nose and pointy ears, with a very wide mouth which he never closed properly, and his teeth were very long and thin – more like needles

139

really. Apart from a scaly body, which was not much bigger than a large potato, the rest of him was just legs. Triple jointed, they were. Four of them had sharp talons but the fifth was really strange: it was like a long thin strip of bone, but one edge was like the teeth of a wood saw.

'You won't last long in this house if you speak to me like that!' he warned, his voice almost a growl now. 'And as for telling Lizzie, you'd just be wasting your time. We're close and snug, just like brother and sister. If ever she needed to choose between you and me, *you'd* be the one whose bones would go into the pot! You're new and still wet behind the ears, so I'll give you just one more chance. But ever behave like that again and you are dead – make no mistake about it!'

That said, Spig leaped from the mantelpiece to the floor and scuttled across the kitchen, leaving a trail of gravy across the flags which I had to clean up after him.

* * *

Later, when Lizzie got back, I decided to tell her what Spig had done anyway.

'Eat up your stew, girl,' Lizzie commanded. 'Need to keep up your strength in our line of work.'

'Don't fancy it much. Old Spig jumped in it and ate some. Put me right off it.'

'Creature needs to eat too. Can't blame him for that. Not his favourite meal though. When he's not after blood, Old Spig likes to eat brains. Human ones are best but he'll make do with sheep and cows. Once he was so desperate he cut off the top of a hedgehog's head and tried to crawl in. Funniest thing you ever saw.'

I couldn't touch the stew; I left Lizzie eating her supper and went to bed early. At the top of the stairs I found someone standing outside my room. It was Nanna Nuckle, and she didn't look happy. She stepped to one side as I reached for the door handle, but then, when I crossed the threshold, gave me a slap across the back of my head so hard that it almost knocked me into the middle of next week.

'What was that for?' I asked angrily as I regained my balance.

'It's for giving me cheek, girl. I won't tolerate cheek!'

With that Nanna Nuckle stomped along the landing to her own room. I hadn't given her cheek, I thought to myself. What on earth was she on about?

CHAPTER 3
NANNA NUCKLE'S HEAD

The following morning Lizzie started to teach me all about plants and herbs. To my surprise, it wasn't just about stopping enemies' hearts or cankering their brains. She taught me about healing too. And some plants were both good and bad.

One of those was called 'mandrake': eating it could make you fall unconscious; too much and you'd never wake up; or it could drive you absolutely mad. But it could also purge poisons and take away the pain from a bad tooth. Lizzie said its roots were shaped like a human body and it shrieked when you dragged it from the ground. I'd have liked to see one of them, but Lizzie said they were rare in the County.

'You never know when this will come in useful, girl,' she told me, pointing to a black-ink sketch of an elder leaf. 'The plant has white flowers and red or blue berries, and can cure rheumatic pain and ease heart problems. It rallies the dying too, giving them new vigour. Once in a while some even make a full recovery. If you or another witch were suffering and close to death, this would revive you.'

I wasn't allowed to write any of this information down though – Lizzie said I had to develop my memory. She said a witch needed to keep most of her spells in her head so she didn't need to waste time looking things up in books again. Lizzie had to go out again that afternoon; she told me to use her library and learn what I could about toadstools.

It wasn't much of a library – just two shelves of mildewed books down in the cellar. I put my candle on the table and looked along the first row, reading the spines. Three of 'em were grimoires covered in cobwebs – books of dark magic spells. I found the book on toadstools and pulled it off the shelf – but then I noticed something else: *Familiars: Good Practice and Bad Habits.*

That sounded a lot more interesting than reading about toadstools. I wanted to find out more about Old Spig, and this was my chance! So I picked up the book and started to leaf through it.

The introductory section was all about the different types of familiar and their suitability for different purposes. I found out that toads were good familiars for old witches who were long past their best, but that water witches in their prime used them all the time because they were suited to a wet and boggy environment.

I also read about how a witch got herself a familiar. You had to tempt it with blood. Most witches started by feeding it from a dish, but some made a small cut on their upper arm and let it suck the blood out directly from their flesh. Eventually, after months of that, a small nipple developed, making it easier for the familiar to draw out the blood. It was a bit like a mother feeding her baby, but really weird. Didn't really want to be a witch, did I? But if it ever happened, I certainly wouldn't be one who used familiar magic.

I flicked through the book faster, trying to find out what Old Spig was. No sign of him at first, but then I came to the last chapter, which was very long. It was called 'The Highest and Most Dangerous Categories of Familiar'.

Lots of strange creatures there, including boggarts and water beasts which I'd already heard of. As for some of the others, I didn't even know that they existed in our world. Maybe some came through portals from the dark, but I didn't have time to read it all and find out.

The opening paragraph contained a warning:

These types of familiar are difficult to control and can present serious dangers to a witch who employs one in her service. Frequently the creature becomes threatening and, over time, the familiar often assumes the dominant role. The witch then becomes the servant.

Then I came to a whole page of sketches. Whoever wrote the book had done a little drawing of each category with the name underneath and a page reference.

Old Spig was there. He was what they called a 'brain guzzler'. I was just turning to the page to find out more when I was suddenly interrupted.

There was a tremendous anguished cry from somewhere upstairs. It sounded like someone had been hurt badly. Lizzie had gone out, so who could it be? Nanna Nuckle?

After the way she'd clouted me the previous night it wouldn't have bothered me if she'd fallen downstairs and broken her blooming neck, but I left the cellar and went to find out what had happened. She wasn't in the kitchen or the gloomy front room. Neither was she lying dead at the bottom of the stairs. A pity, that! So I went up to her room. The door was open and I could see her sitting on a chair next to her bed. I gasped in horror at what I saw. I couldn't believe what had happened to her. It was just too

JOSEPH DELANEY

horrible . . . I started shaking all over.

The top of her head had been sliced off and was hanging forward over her face, held on by just a bit of skin. And the inside of her skull was empty. Old Spig had killed her! He'd guzzled her brains!

I ran down the stairs in a panic, desperate to get as far away as possible. What if Spig was still hungry and he wanted my brains too? I might well be next.

I ran out into the woods and hid amongst the trees, waiting for Lizzie to return. She'd know what to do. Soon it started to rain and I got soaked to the skin, but I was too scared to take shelter back in Lizzie's house.

Lizzie didn't come back until well after dark. I heard her coming through the trees towards the house and rushed to meet her. It was the nearest I ever came to being glad to see her.

'What ails you, girl?' she shouted as I ran towards her.

'Old Spig has killed Nanna Nuckle!' I gasped out. 'He's sliced open the top of her head and eaten her brains!'

Lizzie came to a halt, but instead of being shocked and outraged, she started to laugh. It was loud, wild laughter that could have been heard for miles. Then she grabbed me by the wrist and dragged me back towards the house. We went straight up to Nanna Nuckle's room.

To my surprise, the woman was sleeping in her chair, snoring away, with her head slumped forward onto her chest, her long grey hair hanging down like a dirty curtain almost as far as the floor.

'But I saw it!' I protested. 'She was dead and her head was wide open and her skull was empty.'

Instead of replying, Lizzie stepped forward and eased away the curtain of hair to show a red line around the top of Nanna Nuckle's head.

'Old Spig's inside her head now, fast asleep. I'd show you how cosy he is but it's best not to disturb him. Likes his rest, he does.'

'So he *has* eaten her brains?'

'That's true enough, girl, but it happened long ago. To be truthful, Nanna Nuckle didn't have many brains left to eat. She was getting forgetful and couldn't concentrate. But she was still strong, and that big body can do lots of useful chores for me, like lifting heavy iron pots when I mix up my potions and poisons. So I let Spig guzzle her brains. It's a good arrangement: he finds it cosy inside her head – once inside he can look through her eyes, hear what she hears and talk using her voice. So he uses Nanna Nuckle's body to do heavy work for me. It's a good arrangement. Old Spig spends about half his time in there.'

'But I heard her cry out in pain last night. That's why I went upstairs to her room.'

'Nanna Nuckle isn't there any longer, but when Spig opens up her skull to climb in or out, her body feels the pain and sometimes gives a gasp or even screams if Spig's a bit rough. Anyway, now you know, girl. So take care and do as I say. That big old body is starting to slow down and Old Spig will be looking for a replacement soon. Best make sure it's not you, girl!'

I went to bed, glad to take off my wet clothes. I'd a lot to think about, and I lay there in the dark for hours before finally dropping off to sleep.

That was why Nanna Nuckle had clouted me the other night, I realized. It had been Spig taking his revenge because when he was in the stew I called him a 'dirty little thing'. He was a nasty dangerous creature, and I knew that in order to survive I'd have to sort him out one way or another.

CHAPTER 4
BRAIN PLUGS IN APPLE JUICE

The next four days were uneventful and I was starting to get into a routine. Daytimes were the best because then I saw neither hide nor hair of Old Spig and Nanna Nuckle.

Lizzie liked to sleep in late, and after I'd made her breakfast I'd have a lesson – usually the only one of the day. A lot of it was memory work. She'd make me learn spells by heart and then recite 'em back to her. Later I'd go down into her little library and study the book she'd suggested.

After that I'd go and collect herbs and toadstools before making the main meal of the day. But then it happened . . .

I was making another stew. It was lamb this time. Lizzie had caught and killed one north of Downham and carried it over her shoulders all the way back to her cottage. Wasn't the only thing she'd killed either. I saw the thumb-bones she pulled out of the leather pouch she always wears. They were human, and small too. She'd probably killed a child. It was too horrible to contemplate. I could never do that so it stood to reason that I could never become a bone witch.

Anyway, I was making the stew when Old Spig jumped into it again. This time he didn't even wait until my back was turned. He came over my shoulder from behind and landed slap bang in the middle of it. Gravy splashed up onto my dress, face and hair. It was boiling-hot too and it hurt. And there he was, just his ugly head showing while he slurped away like there was no tomorrow.

I saw red, and before I could bite my tongue I really gave him a telling off.

'Get out of there, you ugly little thing!' I shouted.

'Get out *now*, you greedy, slimy piece of muck! Don't you mess with me!'

Old Spig got out, jumping onto the mantelpiece again. I could see him quivering with anger: his mouth kept opening and closing, showing those sharp little needle-like teeth. It was a long time before he spoke, and when he did, his voice was low and dangerous.

'You're as good as dead,' he told me. 'Brains are best eaten just before the full moon, and that's when I'll eat yours. Soon I'll be sawing the top of your head off. Can't wait to get inside!'

With that, he put the edge of that strange little bone-limb he had against the edge of the wooden mantelpiece. Back and forth he drew it, and that sharp-toothed edge cut through the wood like butter, with the sawdust falling into the hearth. Then he leaped down and was gone, leaving me trembling.

It was just a few days till the full moon. What could I do? I wondered. Tell Lizzie? I decided to do just that, even though I wasn't at all sure she'd help me.

'Old Spig said he's going to eat my brains,' I told

her, just as she was starting to eat her lamb stew.

'Is he now, girl. You must have done something to really annoy him then . . .'

'He jumped in the stew again and I called him names and shouted at him to get out. Threatened me, he did. Said I was as good as dead and that he'd kill me before the full moon.'

Lizzie never even looked at me. She just kept shovelling stew into her mouth.

'Can't you help me?' I asked her at last.

Finally she glanced my way, but her eyes were hard and cruel, with no hint of any kind of sympathy for my plight. 'I'm training you to be a witch so there's one thing you should get into your head now – and that's before Spig's teeth get there!' she said. 'A witch needs to be hard; she needs to survive. This is between you and Old Spig. You got to sort it out one way or the other. Either that or you're not up to the job. Understand?'

I nodded. I would get no help from Lizzie – that much was certain.

'Anyway, tonight you must take yourself up to the dell again. I've buried another little jug close to the roots of that tree. Make sure you have it back here well before dawn. Moon won't help you this time so the digging might just take a little longer.'

That much was true: there was indeed no moon that night. A storm was moving in from the west, the wind bending the tree branches, the whole dell groaning and creaking as if in pain.

Only halfway to the old oak, I was, when Grim Gertrude found me. Moved fast for such an old dead witch who was carrying her head under her arm. Got herself between me and where I wanted to go.

'*Left Lizzie, have you, and come to work with me?*' the pale lips mouthed.

'Ain't ready to do that yet a while,' I told her.

'*No time like the present, girl. You and me would be useful to each other. I could teach you much more than Lizzie – help you lots, I could.*'

It suddenly dawned on me that Gertrude might just be able to help me now. There was no harm in trying. Who else could I turn to?

'Trouble is, Gertrude, I may never be able to work for you. Going to be dead myself soon. Lizzie's familiar, Spig, is going to guzzle my brains. Told me he'd do it before the next full moon. And Lizzie won't help; said I needed to be strong and survive. But I don't know what I can do.'

'*There's always a way, girl, especially when you've got friends like me to help you. Do you know what's in that little jug that Lizzie's sent you to get?*'

'Wouldn't let me see into the last jug I brought her. Told me I'd need a lot of training before I could see into it.'

'*Did she now? Well, inside are prime plugs of young brain, fermenting in apple juice. Whenever Lizzie kills somebody, she takes the thumb-bones but gets bits o' brain for Old Spig as a treat. Doesn't saw the tops off their heads though – got an easier method than that . . . has a special tool she uses. Plunges it right up through the nose and into the*' *skull and cuts out a few choice brain plugs. Brings them back and puts them in that jug with a good lashing of juice. Buries it close to the roots of that tree and leaves it for a few nights to ferment into alcohol. Old Spig loves it. There's lots of magic in this dell that's seeped out of dead witches. That's absorbed by the jug too and gives him extra strength so he can do Lizzie's bidding.'*

'So when I take the jug back he'll be more dangerous than ever?'

'She won't give him the jug until tomorrow night. She'll be going out then so it'll keep him quiet. But what you say's true enough. At first it makes him really sleepy. That would be your time to strike. Kill him while he sleeps. That's your best chance. And it's you or him, so you can't afford to be squeamish. Kill him tomorrow night. That's what I'd do in your place!'

'What's the best way to finish him off?' I asked.

'You could use a sharp knife and chop his little legs off. Couldn't do much then, could he? He'd starve to death slowly. Burying him under a big stone would be best. A very heavy one would finish him off quicker.

158

'Another good reason to do it tomorrow, girl. Big meeting of the three clans then – could last several nights. They're going to curse a spook who works in the south of the County. They want him dead. Done a lot of damage to our sisters down there over the years, he has, so he deserves it all right. Bit of a loner, is Lizzie, but she certainly won't miss something that big. So she'll be out, leaving you alone in the house with Old Spig. So kill him then!'

I'd killed things before, mostly by wringing their necks – chickens, rabbits and hares; you've got to eat, and everybody does that. But killing something that talks – that's different. Didn't like the idea at all. But if I didn't kill Old Spig, then he'd kill me for sure. So I didn't have much choice.

When I got back, I gave Lizzie the jug, then went straight to bed. The following day it rained heavily and Lizzie was quiet and in a right mood. Didn't even bother to give me a lesson – just sat staring into the fire all afternoon, muttering to herself – so I went down to her little library and started reading about familiars again – that last chapter with the section on brain guzzlers.

It didn't tell me much about how to deal with Old Spig. I suppose that's the last thing that crosses most witches' minds. They want to befriend and control a familiar, not kill it. But there was one interesting section on guzzlers' likes and dislikes that told witches about their vulnerabilities.

> *Brain guzzlers can tolerate extreme temperatures but they love boiling liquids, in which they happily immerse themselves for hours at a time.*
>
> *Although they can generally look after themselves, it is important to be aware of some weaknesses that may be exploited by a witch's enemies.*
>
> *The hard, scaly head and body are tough and resistant to the sharpest of blades, but salt is corrosive and burns them. Even if there's insufficient to kill them, it saps their strength and affects their coordination.*
>
> *A blade can also be used to remove their limbs and*

*immobilize them. They are also vulnerable to sunlight
and rarely venture out during the day.*

The line about cutting their limbs off told me that
dead Gertrude knew her stuff all right. That was all the
help I could find in that book, but it was useful to
know about the salt. Not that it was of any immediate
help. Lizzy didn't like the stuff and there wasn't even
a pinch of it in the house.

'I'll be gone for a couple of nights – maybe more,'
Lizzie said that evening as she paused on the doorstep,
looking up at the waxing moon. 'It's the full moon in a
couple of nights. Will you still be here when I get back,
girl? Or will Old Spig be curled up inside your skull?'

With a wicked laugh she set off into the trees. Full of
foreboding, I closed the door and went to the kitchen.
There I sorted through the knife drawer and picked up
the biggest, sharpest one I could find, then started to
climb the stairs.

No point in dawdling. It was best to get it over with.

Lizzie had given Old Spig the jug about an hour before she'd gone out. I hoped he'd still be sleeping . . .

The door of Nanna Nuckle's room was slightly ajar. I opened it just a fraction of an inch and peeped in. She was sitting in her chair, illuminated by a shaft of moonlight, the top of her head hanging forward on that bit of skin. So where was Old Spig?

I heard him before I saw him. There were faint snores coming from the window ledge, so I eased the door open ever so slowly and carefully stepped into the room. There he was, curled up into a ball, most of his legs tucked underneath that ugly head and body of his. I raised the knife and began to tiptoe towards him, one cautious step at a time.

I raised the knife high and prepared to bring it down. Three legs were sticking out. All I had to do was chop them off. He'd probably jump up in pain and fright and then I could slice off the other ones. But I hesitated and my hand began to tremble. To do that in cold blood was horrible. I just couldn't force myself to bring down that knife.

Suddenly both Spig's eyes opened wide and he stared right at me. 'You'd kill me in my sleep, would you?' he said, his voice quiet and dangerous. 'Did you think it'd be that easy? Well, now it's my turn!'

He leaped straight at me. I twisted away but I wasn't fast enough. He landed on top of my head and I felt his claws dig sharply into my scalp. I screamed, dropped the knife and tried to pull him off, but he was tangled up in my hair – and then something even worse happened. I felt him draw that bone-saw across the back of my head; felt it bite into my scalp!

I screamed and fell to my knees. I was terrified. Spig was starting to saw the top of my head off. There was only one thing I could do. One last chance. I crawled over to the wall and butted my head against it as hard as I could. Spig cried out as I squashed his body against the stone. Twice more I did it, then he let go and dropped to the floor, twitching and gasping.

Knew that wasn't the end of him, so I stumbled to my feet and ran out of the room and down the stairs, then out of the house and into the trees. I halted then and looked back, watching the doorway to see if he'd follow me.

Didn't take that long before Spig came after me, but now he was inside Nanna Nuckle's skull. So I kept moving through the trees, further and further from Lizzie's house. Wasn't that worried though. She was big, strong and ugly, and if she got hold of me those big hands could kill me without a doubt; but she had to find and catch me first. Nanna Nuckle wasn't a witch so she couldn't sniff me out.

As long as I kept moving, I'd be safe. And she'd have to be back in her room before dawn. For now the worst was over. But Lizzie would be away for at least another night, and after dark I'd have to face Spig again.

CHAPTER 5
SEVEN BIG HANDFULS

Long before the sun came up, Nanna Nuckle's big body turned and lumbered slowly back towards Lizzie's house. But I was in no hurry to return. I had a lot of thinking to do.

One option was to run away. But where would I go? I'd be welcome at the cottage of my other aunt, Agnes Sowerbutts, but Lizzie would only drag me back again. There was a good chance that she would find me wherever I went. Did she want me dead? Did she want Old Spig to guzzle my brains? What had been the point of training me as a witch if she was going to let Spig kill me? I wondered. Or was that what she'd intended all along? Was I the replacement for

Nanna Nuckle's old body, which was slowing down now?

Get hard and survive, she'd told me. That didn't make sense and contradicted the rest. Did she want me to survive or not? Well, I would do just that. It was me or Spig – one of us was going to die, and it wasn't going to be me. He was vulnerable during the daylight hours and might not think I was brave enough to go back to the house.

That was to my advantage. But what else? *Think, girl!* I told myself. *Use everything you know . . .*

Salt! That would slow him down and affect his coordination. He wouldn't be able to leap onto my head again so easily. But where could I get my hands on some? It was no use looking in any of the local villages. Witches lived there and they were wary of the stuff. None of them used it. I was still only being trained – hopefully I could still touch it. So I needed to go south and get right out of the Pendle district.

Washed myself in a stream first. My hair was matted with blood at the back where Spig had tried to saw my head open. Sore too when I touched it, but the blade hadn't gone very deep. A few tufts of hair came away but I would mend eventually.

I'm not a thief. Never take stuff that doesn't belong to me. But I was desperate. Besides, salt's cheap and I didn't want that much. I saw a farmer and his wife in the distance, working in the fields, so I sneaked into their store. There were big sacks of salt, but I found a bit of cloth and wrapped what I needed in that – seven big handfuls. That done, I set off back towards Lizzie's house.

It was late afternoon when I walked into the kitchen – plenty of time to sort out what I needed. But I went upstairs first to see what was what. Took a knife and a handful of salt, just in case.

Eased open the door of Old Spig's room. Gloomy in there, it was, with the heavy curtains closed. I waited for a few moments for my eyes to adjust, then tiptoed in. Nanna Nuckle was in her usual position in her chair, the top of her head hanging forward, but there was no sign of Spig.

Wasn't daft, was he? He was hiding away some-where until dark. So I had another think. I had to make the best of the situation, and after about half an hour or so I'd worked out what to do.

I went down into the kitchen, made myself a brew and had something to eat. Then I searched Lizzie's house to find the things I needed. She'd no idea of how to keep things tidy and organized so it took me ages. One of the things I found was a meat cleaver – heavier than a knife and just what the doctor ordered.

About an hour before dark I went back up to Spig's room and made my preparations. That done, I became nervous and kept pacing up and down; but then, as it started to get dark, I hid behind the door, the cleaver in my right hand, salt in my left.

Old Spig didn't make much noise when he approached. I could just about hear the tapping of his spindly limbs on the floorboards as he came to the door. I was scared and my hands were trembling, but I couldn't afford to miss. Make a mistake, and a minute later I'd be dead.

At the very last moment he saw me, but it didn't do him any good. I hurled the handful of salt at him. A good shot, it was, and he screamed and started to twitch and writhe, his limbs trying to go in different directions. Then I used the cleaver – but I didn't chop off his legs as Grim Gertrude had advised. He still needed them for what I had planned. I chopped off his bone-saw instead, bringing down the cleaver so hard that it went deep into the floorboards and I couldn't pull it out. Not that it mattered.

After Old Spig had screamed for about a minute he went very quiet and looked up at me. His mouth opened and closed a few times, showing his needle teeth. His legs were still twitching, but I was no longer worried about him jumping onto my head.

'You've maimed me!' he said, his voice all wobbly. 'I'll kill you for that.'

'You said something like that once before,' I told him, 'but I'm still here. Reckon I'll still be here when you're dead and gone! Can't saw my head open now, can you?'

'Not today, I can't, but it won't take long to grow back. Didn't know that, did you? All my limbs grow back eventually. And now I'll make you wish you'd never been born! I'm going to twist your head off your scrawny neck!'

That said, he leaped towards the top of Nanna Nuckle's head, which was exactly what I wanted. No doubt he wanted to use that big body to hurt me good and proper, but he missed and skittered off onto the floor again. Took him five attempts to get inside.

As soon as he managed it, Old Spig started screaming. I'd thrown just one handful of salt at him. That left six more, and I'd put them inside Nanna Nuckle's skull.

Once he was in there, I didn't waste any time. Had to work fast, didn't I? Took the needle and twine I'd found in one of Lizzie's mucky cupboards and stitched the top of the skull to the bottom. Wasn't a very tidy job but I used lots of stitches and made them really tight. Nanna Nuckle twitched a lot and saliva started to dribble down her chin while I did it, but she didn't groan as she had when I'd poured the salt in. Old Spig was trapped inside – I didn't think his bone-saw would grow back fast enough to save him.

When I went back the following morning, Nanna Nuckle was very still. She looked dead. Couldn't tell whether Old Spig was still alive inside her skull, but when I put my ear really close there were no sounds. Of course, it didn't help that I'd pulled the curtains right back and a shaft of bright sunlight was shining straight into her face. Wasn't over yet though, was it? I still had to face Lizzie and tell her what I'd done.

I was sitting on a stool in front of the fire when Lizzie came home. It was late afternoon.

'You still here?' she asked. 'Thought you'd be dead by now.'

'It's Old Spig that's dead,' I replied. 'I killed him.'

'Pull my other leg,' she said; 'it's got bells on it!'

'Ain't joking,' I told her. 'He's upstairs . . .'

Lizzie must have read in my face that I was telling

171

the truth because she sort of twisted her mouth like she does when she's angry, grabbed me by the wrist and dragged me upstairs. She peered closely at Nanna Nuckle, and then, with her forefinger, traced the jagged line of stitches across that broad forehead, then put her nose very close and, after sniffing three times, shook her head.

'What I can't understand is why he didn't just saw his way out,' she muttered. Then her eyes drifted across to the place behind the door and she noticed the cleaver still sticking out of the floorboards and Old Spig's little bone-saw lying on the floor. The stump was red with his blood.

'I threw salt at him and put more inside the skull. When he jumped into it, I stitched him up.'

Lizzie didn't say anything for a long time; she just kept staring at the top of Nanna Nuckle's head.

'It was him or me. You told me I'd to sort it one way or the other or I wouldn't be up to the job. Well, I sorted it, didn't I?'

'Get hold of her legs, girl. I'll take the shoulders,'

Lizzie said. 'Can't leave 'em here or they'll start to rot.'

So we buried them out in the woods. One grave, two bodies – not that you'd notice. After that I walked back to the house with Lizzie, not sure what would happen next. I was past being scared. At that moment, after all I'd done, I didn't care one jot what happened to me.

We sat in front of the fire and it was a long time before Lizzie spoke.

'In a way, girl, you did me a favour,' she said, staring into the flames. 'Using a familiar as strong as Old Spig is dangerous. The longer it goes on, the more they start to get the upper hand. In the end I was killing when I didn't need fresh bones. Just doing it to keep him happy and stocked up with his favourite tipple – brain plugs in apple juice.

'He was starting to control me, and when it gets like that it's best for a witch to put an end to it and get herself a new familiar. But me and Old Spig were close, and I just couldn't bring myself to do him in. So I was half hoping that you might do the job for me. And you

173

did well, girl. You remind me of myself when I was a girl of your age. You could almost be my daughter . . .' she said, giving me a wicked smile.

So that was it. I'd survived my first two weeks with Bony Lizzie. And that was what I was going to do in the future. Wasn't going to drink people's blood or take their bones, but I was willing to learn all the tricks that would keep me safe from other witches – and anyone else who tried to harm me.

I'm going to survive. You can be sure of that. It's as certain as my name's Alice Deane.

THE BANSHEE
WITCH

CHAPTER 1
A HARD LESSON

The enemy before me was big, strong and ruthless. This was dangerous and I couldn't afford to make a mistake. He clasped a long knife in his right hand and a heavy club in his left and was eager to use them.

With a roar of anger, he charged straight at me, swinging his club in an arc from right to left. I managed to block it, but the force of the impact jarred my arm and shoulder so badly that I almost dropped my staff. I groaned and twisted away, retreating clockwise.

We were in a ruined building, an old tavern long abandoned to the elements. I'd been chased through the woods and, thinking I'd shaken my pursuer off my trail, had taken refuge here. It was a big mistake: now I was in serious trouble.

We were fighting in a confined space, down in a large, gloomy cellar with only one door. Steps led upwards, but he was standing between me and my escape route. I feinted with my staff, and when he responded to block it, I changed the direction of my swing and made contact with his right temple. It was a good strong blow and he dropped to one knee. I hit him again – a hard crack on his shoulder. Then I ran for it – up the steps and towards the open door.

There was a thud as the knife buried itself in the woodwork to my left, just a few inches from my shoulder. Then he was pounding up the steps after me, getting nearer with every stride. I almost made it through the door, but then he jumped on me from behind, bringing me down hard, flat on my face. His right arm came across my windpipe and started to press. I'd just time to suck in a quick breath before I began to choke.

I struggled, kicking my legs and twisting my body, but it was no good. I was still gripping my staff with my left hand, but from that prone position couldn't use it. My eyes were darkening. He was strangling the life out of me . . .

So I rapped three times on the top step with my right hand. Instantly my assailant relinquished the choker-hold and stood up. I stumbled to my feet, my head spinning, but feeling happy just to be able to breathe again.

'Not one of your best days, Master Ward!' he said, shaking his head. 'Never take refuge in any room that's only got one door! Mind you, you did get in a couple of good blows with your staff. But never turn your back on an enemy with a knife. I could have stuck it in the back of your neck with my eyes shut!'

I bowed my head and said nothing, but I knew there was no chance he would have put the knife into me from behind. His job was to train me, not kill me. I'd taken my chance of escape and had come close to succeeding.

I'm a spook's apprentice, being trained to deal with all manner of things that come out of the dark, such as ghosts, ghasts, boggarts and witches. Facing me was a large, shaven-headed man called Bill Arkwright. My master, John Gregory, had seconded me to him for training in the physical skills needed by a spook: fighting with staffs; unarmed combat; hunting and tracking.

Picking up my staff, I followed him out of the house; soon we were on the canal bank, heading back to the dilapidated old mill which was his home. Arkwright was the spook who looked after the County north of Caster. He specialized in things that came out of the lakes, marshes and canals of this region – water witches mainly, but there were also all manner of weird beasts, such as wormes, selkies, skelts and kelpies to contend with, some of which I'd never seen except in the Bestiary, the big book of creatures of the dark which my master, John Gregory, had illustrated with his own hand.

Recently we'd defeated the water witch, Morwena,

and now Mr Gregory had set off back to his house at Chipenden without me. The final months of my training with Bill Arkwright were proving to be the hardest I'd ever experienced. I was covered in bruises from head to foot. The practice sessions when we fought with staffs were brutal, with no quarter given. But I was sharpening my skills; slowly starting to improve.

Arkwright's mill had once been haunted by the ghosts of his mam and dad; trapped there despite all his efforts to release them. That had made him bitter, driving him to drink. But recently I'd helped him to liberate them and they had gone to the light. As a result, Arkwright had slowly changed, a lot of his pain and anger dissipating. Now he drank rarely and his temper was much better. I still preferred John Gregory as my master, but Bill Arkwright was teaching me well, and despite his rough ways, I was learning to respect him.

But Arkwright was still a very hard man. John Gregory kept live witches imprisoned in pits

181

indefinitely. Bill Arkwright confined them as a punishment for a limited time. Then he killed them, cutting out their hearts so that they couldn't return from the dead. He was a good spook but I knew him to be ruthless.

It was misty on the towpath, and before we came within sight of the large tethering post on the canal bank outside the mill, we heard the bell. Three rings indicated that it was spook's business, so Arkwright picked up the pace and I followed close at his heels.

A middle-aged woman was standing beneath the huge bell. She wore a dark wide-brimmed hat pulled low over her eyes, black stockings and sturdy leather shoes with flat heels. I thought she looked like a servant from a big house and I was soon proved right.

'Good day to you, sir,' she said, giving a little curtsey. 'Would you by any chance be Mister Arkwright?'

I tried to keep a straight face. Bill was wearing

his cloak with the hood up against the damp and carrying his big staff with its twelve-inch blade and six backward-facing barbs. Quite clearly he was the local spook.

'Aye, I'm Bill Arkwright,' he replied. 'What brings you here on a cold damp winter afternoon?'

'Mistress Wicklow of Lune Hall has sent me. She'd like to see you as soon as possible. We've heard a banshee wailing two nights in a row and we're all frit to death! The gardener saw it on the lakeside near the narrow bridge. It was washing a burial shroud in the water – which means someone is going to die soon—'

'Let me be the judge of that,' Arkwright said.

'My mistress thinks it'll be her husband . . .'

Arkwright raised one eyebrow. 'Is he in good health at present?'

'Fell off his horse in the autumn and broke a leg. Got pneumonia soon after and it's left him with a bad cough. Mistress says he's not the man he was. Getting worse by the hour . . .'

'Tell your mistress I'll be there before dark.'

The servant gave another little curtsey, and with a muttered thanks turned north and set off down the towpath.

'It's a waste of time, really,' Arkwright said as we watched her disappear into the mist. 'There's nothing a spook can do about a banshee. They forecast deaths but don't bring them about.'

'Mr Gregory doesn't even think they do that,' I said. 'He doesn't believe anybody can see into the future.'

'Do you agree with him, Master Ward?'

'Witches are able to scry, I'm sure of it. The things they prophesy can happen. I've seen it with my own eyes.'

'Your master would just say it was coincidence,' Arkwright said, rubbing the top of his bald head, 'but I'm sure that you and I are both of the same mind. There's got to be something in it. Some people and some entities, including a banshee, can see what's going to happen in the future. So I think it's very likely that Master Wicklow or somebody else in that house will be dead before the end of the week. But it won't be the banshee that actually does the killing. It's sensed a coming death, that's all.'

'So why are we going then? Why get involved?'

Arkwright frowned. 'People expect us to help; they feel better if we're around in situations like this. Think how many times a doctor repeatedly visits the bedside of a dying man when he's unable to do anything – sometimes not even to relieve the pain. But he visits anyway because it makes the patient and his family feel better.

'And we have a second reason for going. We need the money. Clients have been few and far between recently. I've killed water witches, but nobody has paid me for it. Our larder is bare, Master Ward, and although they're easy enough to catch, we don't want to eat fish every day. Up at that big house they pay good money to local tradesmen. They can well afford it, so we might as well have our share.

'And there's a third reason if the first two aren't enough for you. An apprentice should see and hear a banshee if there's one about. It's part of your training to learn the limitations of a spook. As I said, we can do nothing about 'em!'

CHAPTER 2
THE SHROUD WASHER

Carrying our bags and staffs, we set off within the hour, heading north. Normally we would have taken Claw, the big wolfhound that Arkwright used to hunt water witches through the marshes, but she was expecting pups and would give birth any day now.

'Let's hope they give us a bite of supper and a hot drink,' Arkwright growled as we left the canal and headed north-east through the trees. 'It's a miserable damp night to keep watch.'

We hadn't been walking much more than half an hour when we saw a figure jump over a stile and head our way down the towpath. It was a red-faced farmer, striding towards us in big muddy boots. He looked

187

very worried, as if carrying the weight of the whole world on his shoulders.

'Here comes trouble!' Arkwright said, keeping his voice low as the man approached. 'Not known for paying his bills, is Farmer Dalton. Half the tradesmen in the district are chasing him!'

'Thank goodness I've caught you, Mr Arkwright!' he said, blocking our path. 'Three sheep have been taken in one night. In the west pasture. The one next to the marsh.'

'Taken? Do you mean missing, eaten or drained?' Arkwright asked.

'Drained of blood.'

'Big wounds or small?'

'Deep puncture marks on their necks and backs.'

'Three in one night, you say? Well, it's not a ripper boggart or their bellies would be cut open – most likely a water witch is to blame. Though for them to take animals is rare. It suggests the witch is injured and can't get human prey. In that case she could be very dangerous – might even approach the farmhouse.'

'I've young children . . .'

'Well, they'll be safe enough as long as you keep all your doors and windows secure. I'll sort it but I expect to be paid.'

'Won't have money until after the first spring market . . .'

'I can't wait that long,' Arkwright said firmly. 'I'll take mutton and cheese in direct payment. A week's supply. Is that a deal?'

The farmer nodded but clearly wasn't pleased at having to cough up payment so soon.

'I'll be there soon after dark,' said Arkwright. 'I've another job to attend to first.'

The farmer soon left us, climbing back over the stile to head for his farm, now clearly really worried that his family might be at risk.

The mist thickened, hampering our progress, and we didn't reach the manor house much before dark. Lune Hall was big, with a fancy turret, and was set in extensive grounds. Approaching it from the west, I

189

could see a lake to the rear, with a small island at its centre, connected to the main garden by a narrow ornamental bridge. Beyond the lake was what looked like an ancient mound.

'Is that a burial mound?' I asked. 'A barrow?'

'Indeed it is, Master Ward. Some say it's the last resting place of an important Celtic chieftain.'

The Celts were the race who arrived in the County as the native 'Little People' were starting to decline. Centuries later, they sailed west across the sea to the large island called Ireland and made that their home.

I turned my attention back to the large and imposing house. Only lords, ladies, knights and esquires would be admitted through the front door of such an establishment, so Arkwright led us round the back to the tradesmen's entrance. After he'd knocked twice, the door was opened by the same maid who'd made the journey to the mill. She showed us into the kitchen and, without being asked, brought us each a bowl of hot soup and some generous slices of bread, thickly buttered. We sat at the table and tucked in. When we'd finished, she led us along a gloomy wood-panelled corridor and out into a small flagged yard to the rear, where a small woman in a dark, well-tailored coat and sturdy walking shoes was waiting.

'This is Mr Arkwright, ma'am,' said the maid, who immediately turned and went back into the house, leaving us alone with her mistress.

'Good evening, Mr Arkwright,' said the woman, giving us a warm smile. 'Is this your apprentice?'

Her accent told me that she originated from Ireland. Long ago, when I visited the Topley market with my dad, there were lots of horse traders there from that country. They used to race their mounts up and down the muddy lanes.

'It is that, ma'am,' Bill Arkwright replied, giving a little bow. 'His name is Tom Ward.'

'Well, thank you both for coming so promptly,' she said. 'I do fear that my husband's life is in danger. His cough is worsening by the hour.'

'Has the doctor attended him?' asked Arkwright.

'To be sure, he comes twice a day but can find no

explanation for my husband's very sudden deterioration. He had recovered fully from the pneumonia. There's no reason for him to get worse now. I fear the banshee has marked him for death. I'm just hoping that you can do something to save him. Follow me – I'll show you where she appears.'

It was still winter, so the garden was not at its best. Even so, you could tell that in spring and summer it would really be something special. It was subdivided into many sections, the path weaving its way through wicker archways and bowers sheltered by stone ivy-clad walls. The shrubs and ornamental trees gradually started to give way to larger species of oak and ash as the garden merged naturally into a wood.

We followed Mistress Wicklow down the long garden path towards the bridge that crossed the lake to give access to the island.

'In my country, *banshee* means "woman of the fay folk",' she said, glancing back at us over her shoulder. 'A fay is what you'd call a fairy in the County . . .'

'We don't believe in goblins and fairies, ma'am,' Arkwright told her. 'We have enough to contend with without them!'

'I'm sure you do, Mr Arkwright, but this threat is real enough. Matthew, my gardener, has seen her and I've heard her. 'Tis a terrible scream, enough to curdle the blood. Anyway, here is Matthew – he is waiting for us now . . .'

Matthew stepped forward out of the gloom and touched his cap in respect. He was old and weather-beaten, long past his prime. It must have been hard for him to keep up the hard physical work of gardener to such a big house.

'Tell them what you saw, Matthew,' Mistress Wicklow commanded.

The gardener nodded and shivered. 'It was yonder,' he said, pointing towards the lake. 'I was standing on the narrow bridge thinking how the lilies wanted thinning out when I saw her kneeling on the bank—'

'On this shore or on the island?' Arkwright interrupted.

'This shore, sir. She was kneeling right on the edge of the lake, washing something in the water. It looked like a burial shroud to me. The moon was shining brightly and I could see that the material was covered in dark stains. I was scared; fixed to the spot. I couldn't tear my gaze away. She kept dipping the shroud into the water, then wringing it out, but the stains were still there. The water was darkening each time, but she couldn't wash it clean.

'Then she turned her head and looked straight at me. Gave a terrible wailing cry that almost killed me stone-dead on the spot. A second later she disappeared, but I'll never forget her.'

'What did she look like? Was she young or old?' my master asked.

'That was the surprising thing, sir. She was young and really pretty. It was hard to believe that such a terrible cry could be uttered by such a comely mouth.'

'Well, ma'am, we'll stay here tonight and keep watch,' Arkwright told Mistress Wicklow. 'I suggest that nobody approaches this part of the garden for at least twenty-four hours. By then we should know what's what.'

'Then I'll leave everything in your hands,' she said. 'I have faith in you, Mr Arkwright. You look strong and dependable. If anyone can save my husband's life, it'll be you.'

Arkwright bowed, and with a little smile for both of us, Mistress Wicklow turned and walked back towards the house.

I looked at my temporary master. I wondered if he had forgotten all about the farmer he'd promised to help with the water witch that evening. I was about to ask him about it when he looked at me and shook his head. 'I fear there's nothing to be done here,' he said sadly. 'If Mistress Wicklow's husband is going to die, he'll die, and there's nothing you or I can do about it. But there's no point me telling her that.'

I wasn't happy with Arkwright's attitude. John Gregory would have told her the truth, but it wasn't worth saying anything to him. My new master was a law unto himself. And he soon answered my question about the farmer.

'Well, Master Ward, I'll be off to deal with the water witch but should be back sometime tomorrow. Probably best if they think I'm keeping watch too. It means that when you go to the kitchen at dawn, they'll give you two breakfasts to bring back here. Aren't you a lucky lad?'

'Looks like being a long cold night first,' I grumbled. I didn't like the idea of misleading Mistress Wicklow.

But he simply shrugged and told me, 'You've got the easy job! Forget all that fairies and fays nonsense – a banshee is just an elemental, and a low-level one at that. And this one's pretty with it! What more could you want? She can't hurt you, so get as close as you can and see what she's about.'

With that, Arkwright gave me a wink, headed for the edge of the garden and pushed through the hedge to rejoin the lane.

* * *

Soon the mist began to lift and the large disc of the moon rose over the trees. It was waning, two days beyond full, but it cast a strong silver light over the garden.

I decided to keep watch from the bridge. At first I stood leaning against the wooden rail, but finally I grew weary and settled myself down cross-legged on the boards, my staff in my left hand, my bag close by me. I kept nodding off and waking up suddenly, so finally I lay down on my back and rested my head on my bag. Then I closed my eyes.

Had Bill Arkwright been here, we'd have taken it in turns to keep watch while the other slept. But what did it matter in this case? The banshee couldn't actually hurt anyone, and if it appeared on the lake shore, its cry would wake me up instantly. So I allowed myself to fall asleep.

But suddenly I awoke. Something was wrong . . . A cold feeling was running the length of my spine – the one that warned me when something from the dark was close. I seized my staff and got quickly to my feet.

Instantly I heard a terrible wail, which made me shiver and shake. No animal or bird of the night could utter such a terrifying sound – I knew it had to be the banshee.

That unnerving cry seemed to have come from the far side of the lake. I decided to go and take a closer look as my master had instructed, so I left the bridge and began to follow the shore anticlockwise, heading for the source of that chilling scream. There were lots of shrubs and trees close to the lake – mainly willows with long trailing branches. The ground was boggy underfoot so my progress was slow.

Again I heard the wail of the banshee, this time much closer. It stopped me dead in my tracks. Arkwright had said that a banshee wasn't dangerous, but that cry suggested otherwise, and the hairs on the back of my neck were beginning to rise.

And then I saw her . . .

She had her back to me and was kneeling in the mud right on the very edge of the water.

Arkwright had advised me to get a really close look.

Why not? She couldn't harm me, he'd said. So I took a cautious step nearer, then another one. Yes, she was washing something in the lake. And the gardener had been right. It certainly looked like the shroud they wrapped a corpse in before nailing it inside the coffin. I moved closer still. The figure had her back to me and I could see stains spreading in the water like black ink.

Blood from the shroud? It certainly looked like it. And what was it that I'd read in the Spook's Bestiary? Blood on the banshee shroud meant that a violent death was being foretold.

But Mr Wicklow was ill with worsening congestion of the lungs, perhaps resulting from pneumonia. So that didn't fit – unless someone else in the house was going to die violently.

I took another couple of steps. Then I became aware of something else . . .

Perched on a branch directly above the banshee I saw a large black crow. It seemed to be staring directly at me. I shivered. There was something baleful and malevolent about that bird.

Suddenly the banshee pulled the shroud out of the water and started to wring it dry. At the same time she wailed for a third time, a cry so terrible and intense that I held my breath until it was finished and felt myself trembling all over.

The cry stopped as quickly as it had begun, and she carried on twisting the shroud as if determined to wring every last drop of moisture from it. While she was thus occupied, I took another step towards her. That was a mistake. A twig cracked under my foot and the banshee turned her head and looked directly at me.

My mouth suddenly grew dry and my whole body started to tremble. The cold feeling down my spine was suddenly much more intense. The gardener had been right about the burial shroud but wrong about the banshee's face.

It was hideous – pitted and cracked like the surface of a dry lake bed in high summer. The eyes were just two dark holes. She opened her mouth wide, but instead of that blood-curdling wail, the banshee hissed at me like an angry cat. No doubt she meant to terrify me, but I stood my ground, gazing directly into that horrible face.

I expected the water elemental to disappear, but to my surprise, she got to her feet. And then she spoke.

'Be gone, boy! Don't linger here or you'll be dead!'

No sooner had she uttered those words than the black crow flapped its wings and took flight.

I didn't think banshees spoke. They were known only for their terrible wail. Now she began to move away from me along the lake shore, walking quickly. I followed, but as I passed the place where she'd been washing the shroud, a shaft of moonlight showed me footprints in the mud. She was barefoot. Not only that: I could hear the sound of squelching feet moving away from me. This wasn't a banshee, I was sure of it, because they weren't solid. But what exactly was I dealing with? Some sort of witch? Had that black crow been her familiar? Mouldheel witches went barefoot. Surely there wasn't one here?

She started to run and I gave chase. Now I regretted leaving my silver chain in my bag – I could have cast it ahead of me and brought her down. I hadn't thought I'd be dealing with something solid that ran so quickly. She was beginning to widen the gap between us. And there, directly ahead, right at the edge of the trees, was the burial mound. She made straight for it and was now out in the open, while I was still hampered by trees. There was a sudden flash of bright light directly ahead. It blinded me momentarily, and I almost ran into a low branch, grazing it with my head. Then I burst out of the trees. I was in the open too now, but there was no sign of the banshee.

I stopped and looked about me. Nothing. Then I approached the grassy mound cautiously. It was roughly oval in shape, and on the side nearest me rose up quite steeply in an almost vertical wall. I looked down and saw the footprints in the mud. They led right up to the earthen wall. It was as if the witch had suddenly disappeared. Either that or somehow run right into the mound . . .

Puzzled, I did one full circuit of the mound and then headed back through the trees towards the ornamental bridge. Once there, I settled down for the night again, wrapped in my cloak with my head resting on my bag. It was very cold and my sleep was fitful. I kept thinking over what had happened. What was going on? This certainly wasn't a banshee we were facing – not according to what I'd read. I had a lot to tell Bill Arkwright.

By dawn I was pacing back and forth across the bridge, deciding whether or not it was too early to go to the kitchen and ask for my breakfast. Perhaps I would get two as Arkwright had suggested. Why not? I was certainly hungry enough. Thinking I'd waited long enough, I was just about to set off for the house when I heard footsteps in the lane and Bill Arkwright forced his way through the hedge and back into the garden. I started – I hadn't expected him back so soon.

As soon as I saw his face, I groaned inwardly. He was leaning heavily on his staff and walking with a pronounced roll of his shoulders. He looked very angry. What was worse, his lips were stained purple. He'd been drinking red wine. He did so only rarely these days, but it never helped his mood.

'Shall I go and get us some breakfast?' I suggested as he approached the bridge.

'Breakfast? You can forget about that, Master Ward. It's the last thing I want. I should have gone straight to the farm instead of bringing you here to see this blessed banshee.'

'It's not—' I began, about to tell him what I'd discovered, but his face instantly darkened with anger.

'Shut your mouth! Just listen for once!' he roared. 'It was a worme, not a water witch, and a blooming big one at that. It got into the farmhouse and killed a child! Blood and bone!' he cursed. 'A child died because I came here.'

I bowed my head, not knowing what to say.

'We're going back there right away. It's holed up somewhere in an old boathouse and it'll take two of us to flush it out. A very dangerous thing is a worme. So come on, let's waste no time or it'll kill again.'

With those words he led us back onto the lane, and soon we were hurrying along towards the canal and the farm beyond it – the banshee far from our thoughts.

CHAPTER 3
THE WORME

A cold wind was blowing in from the sea, so I pulled up my hood to keep my ears warm. I lagged behind Arkwright for most of the way, knowing of old that he was not in the mood for company and that the only words I'd hear would be curses. But once we'd crossed the canal and were on the track that led to the farm, he beckoned me forward to walk alongside him.

'Listen carefully, Master Ward, because what I say might just save your life. I'm going to tell you what I know about wormes – which, as you know, are spelled with an *e* at the end to set them apart from ordinary earthworms. Some have legs, most have tails, and all are vicious and very bad-tempered. I saw the tracks the creature made in the mud: this one has legs *and* a tail. The legs'll give it speed, so watch out!'

The thought of facing such a danger made me feel nervous. Arkwright hadn't been prepared to risk tackling it alone, so this was clearly going to be a very hazardous job.

'Their bodies are eel-like but covered with very tough green scales like armour plates, which are very difficult to penetrate with a blade,' he went on. 'And as for their jaws, they're long, with a mouth full of razor-sharp fangs that can easily bite off a head or an arm. Wormes are very dangerous creatures, Master Ward – they can be the size of a small dog or as big as a horse. This one is bigger than me – surprisingly big to stray this far south, away from the lakes. That's where they are usually to be found.

'When they catch a human, they usually kill their victim by squeezing him to death before eating him, bones and all, leaving hardly a trace. But with animals such as cattle, they just bite deeply and suck out the blood. That's what this one did with the sheep – that's why I made the mistake of thinking it was a water witch. A mistake that cost a young boy's life. It got into the house and dragged him from his bed. When the farmer went upstairs to check on the boy before going to bed himself, it was already too late. The worme had eaten him. All that remained was blood-stained fragments of his nightshirt.'

What Arkwright had described was terrible and sad. I felt really sorry for the parents. No wonder my master was angry, but it was a mistake that any spook could have made.

'Some people call them dragons,' Arkwright continued. 'That's because they breathe out clouds of steam to confuse their prey. It hides them while they spit. That spit is poisonous and can kill a fully-grown man in just minutes. If it makes contact with your skin, you're as good as dead. If it even touched your breeches or shirt, it would soak through in seconds, still probably delivering a lethal dose. But with two of us on the attack it'll be confused. It won't know which of us to tackle first and that'll give us a better chance of dealing with it. Any questions?'

'Will I be able to use my silver chain against it?'

Arkwright shook his head. 'You'd be wasting your time, Master Ward. Despite those scales, it's sinuous and slippery and would soon wriggle clear of it. No, it's immune to silver and to salt. We use our staffs. That's the safest and surest way. Let me deal with it directly while you approach it from one side; keep some distance between us to confuse it – then it won't be absolutely sure where the main threat will come from. Hopefully I'll be able to get in close and finish it off before it can do me any serious damage.'

As we passed the farmhouse, we heard a woman wailing inside – no doubt the poor mother who'd lost her young son. We continued down the narrow muddy track, which led to a water channel and then ran alongside it. We were now passing through a marsh and approaching the sea. There was little water in the channel at that moment, but it was tidal and allowed small boats access to the sea. A number of wooden boathouses were dotted along its edges, and Arkwright stopped outside the largest. The building was as big as a barn but dilapidated and fallen into disrepair. I saw that the clasp on the small door was fastened with a coil of barbed wire.

'Well, here we are,' Arkwright said. 'This is the place I tracked it to. Let's hope it's still lurking in here. It's likely to stay here because it's fed recently and will remain under cover until it next goes hunting again – probably after dark tonight. Let's check before we go in . . .'

Arkwright circled the boathouse warily. Around us the marsh grass was bent and twisted; it danced to the dictates of the wind. The landscape was flat and bleak, with mudflats in the distance. It seemed totally deserted, but for the seabirds far above descending in long slow spirals out of the grey winter sky.

'There! Can you see the tracks? That's where it went in . . .'

On the channel side of the boathouse there was a mud slope that led from a huge door down to the water. This was where boats were launched. There were clawed tracks, smeared in places where the worme's tail had slicked across the mud. The door was rotten, with most of the planks broken away near the bottom, leaving a jagged lower edge. The creature had squeezed itself in underneath.

We completed the circuit and Arkwright nodded in satisfaction. 'No fresh tracks, Master Ward, so it's still here. Light a candle. It'll be dark in there . . .'

I pulled a candle-stub from my pocket and got the tinderbox from my bag. I had to crouch low near the door and shield both from the cold wind, but in moments I'd managed to light the wick.

'Ready?' Arkwright asked.

I nodded. It took Arkwright just seconds to twist the wire free of the clasp across the small door; then he stepped inside cautiously, his staff at the ready. I followed close behind, protecting the flickering candle as best I could.

The moment I entered, I knew that the worme was lurking nearby. The whole area was filled with a dense warm mist that had a noxious, acrid stink, making my eyes water. It was the breath of the creature. No wonder some people confused wormes with dragons, thinking that they breathed fire.

The rotting hulk of a boat filled most of the space inside. It was supported by wooden beams, three feet or more above the earthen floor, and something large scuttled out towards us from the darkness beneath.

I caught a glimpse of a wide mouth full of sharp, murderous teeth. Then most of the worme came into view. It was big all right. Had it been able to stand upon its hind legs, it would have been taller than Arkwright, and the tail trailing behind it added another third to that. But its legs were stubby and the large toes were webbed and armed with sharp curved talons, so that its body was almost scraping the earth.

As Arkwright had told me, it had green scales covering its long body.

With a sudden loud hiss, the worme breathed out, and a large plume of steam erupted from its nostrils, making it difficult to see. Arkwright jabbed downwards at it with his staff. He missed the head by inches and it scampered backwards until the rear half of its body was once more under the hulk of the boat. It snarled up at us, its small eyes glittering in the candlelight.

'Stand back, Master Ward. I'll deal with this,' Arkwright said, moving forward and readying the blade of his staff.

Suddenly the creature spat, and Arkwright quickly stepped to one side, just in time to avoid the large globule of dark liquid that had been aimed at his legs.

'Keep your distance,' he advised, gesturing me back with his right arm. 'Remember what I said about worme-spit! If the venom touches your skin, you could be dead within minutes. Pass me the candle, then move away to the left.'

I handed him the candle and he held it high. The worme seemed to move its head and stare towards the light, but then it twisted back to face Arkwright and breathed out another plume of mist. Next, hidden by that cloud, it hissed and spat again: a thick ball of slime landed on Arkwright's right boot. Luckily the boot leather would be too thick to be penetrated; it was a good job it hadn't landed on his trousers.

Again Arkwright moved the candle. 'The light fascinates it . . .' he said softly. 'It's a good idea to distract its attention. Now you move a little closer and threaten it with your staff. Not too close, mind!'

I did as he commanded, thrusting my staff towards it. Its eyes were on me now and then, in a fury, his staff raised, Arkwright suddenly rushed in to attack the ugly creature. He brought the blade down hard, three times in quick succession. The first blow missed as the beast twisted away, but the second and third blows struck home and the long blade went deep into its head and neck. It thrashed and writhed, sliding back into the darkness under the boat. Its blood was dark and thick, a viscous slime oozing out onto the ground.

Arkwright handed the candle back to me. 'Crouch down and give me as much light as possible,' he ordered.

Then he put down his staff, fished a long-bladed knife from his bag and crawled under the boat. By the light of the candle I watched him stabbing the creature again and again until it gave a great gasp and lay still.

'Not quite as difficult as I'd thought,' he remarked when, once more, he was standing beside me. 'Well, Master Ward, let's go and tell Farmer Dalton the job's done . . .'

In answer to Arkwright's triple rap, the farmer came to the front door. I saw that his eyes were red and swollen with grief.

'The beast's body is lying in the biggest of the boatyards yonder and soon it'll start to rot,' Arkwright said, gesturing towards the salt marsh. 'It'll need

215

attending to. I have urgent business elsewhere now.'

The farmer nodded and gave a great sob that shook his whole body.

'I'm sorry for the loss of your son,' Arkwright said respectfully.

The man nodded but couldn't speak.

'Well, erm, we'd best be on our way,' continued my master.

'Wait! You'll want paying,' said the farmer. 'Forget the mutton and cheese – I do have a little emergency money in the attic . . .'

'No payment is required,' my master said. 'Put it towards the funeral expenses.'

With that, we were on our way east again, heading back towards the Wicklows' residence. For a while we walked in silence, keeping up a steady pace, but then I remembered the strange business of the banshee.

'The banshee, Mr Arkwright . . .'

'The banshee, indeed, Master Ward. We really do need to be seen to sort that banshee now. We must hope they pay us well for our trouble. I hadn't the heart to take anything from Dalton after what happened.'

'But it wasn't a banshee, Mr Arkwright. At least, I don't think so . . .'

Arkwright came to a sudden halt and glared at me. 'Did you see it?' he demanded.

I nodded.

'Was she as pretty as the gardener said?'

I shook my head.

'Well, he was an old man. To a man of his age any woman looks pretty!'

'She was hideous. Her skin was cracked and disfigured.'

'Was she washing a burial shroud?'

'It was covered in blood and there were big dark stains in the water – that predicts a violent death, doesn't it? Yet Master Wicklow is suffering from congestion of the lungs . . .'

Arkwright rubbed the top of his head and frowned. 'So what makes you think it wasn't a banshee?'

JOSEPH DELANEY

'She left footprints in the mud at the water's edge. Banshees don't leave footprints, do they? That type of elemental is just a spirit. And she spoke to me. Warned me off. Said if I lingered, I'd be dead. Then she set off through the trees . . .'

As I spoke, I heard her voice in my memory and I realized something that I'd thought nothing of at the time. 'She had the same accent as Mistress Wicklow. She was from Ireland, the big island across the water . . .'

'Was she now? So what happened then, Master Ward. Did you obey her?'

'No. I followed her. I was running as fast as I could but I didn't catch her. She sprinted towards the burial mound and disappeared. Her footprints went right up to it. It was as if she'd vanished.'

'Really?' said Arkwright, scratching his head. 'Well, that's interesting.'

'And just before that there was a flash of bright light,' I continued. 'I think she was a witch. There was a black crow on a branch just above her while she was washing the shroud. Could that have been her familiar?'

Arkwright looked thoughtful and perhaps a little worried. 'Come on, Master Ward, let's continue on our way. I'll have to think about this for a while . . .'

So we went on towards Lune Hall, my master silent and deep in thought.

CHAPTER 4
THE CELTIC ASSASSIN

It was getting dark again by the time we reached the hall, but the sky was clear and the moon would soon be up.

'Right, Master Ward, we need to talk,' Arkwright said, stepping off the track, placing his bag and staff on the ground and leaning back against a tree trunk. 'It's been a long day and our bellies must be thinking our throats have been cut. I *was* going to suggest we get ourselves a bite to eat, but we can't risk that now. We need to follow the advice that John Gregory gave us, and fast before facing the dark. Because I think we're about to step into unknown territory. Ever heard of the Celtic witches?'

I put down my own staff and bag and frowned, searching my memory. 'I'm not sure whether the Spook's Bestiary has an entry on them or not – if so, it's very short.'

'Exactly, Master Ward, because not a lot's known about them. They mostly come from the south-western region of Ireland. That whole island is shrouded in mystery. Some call it the Emerald Isle because it gets even more rainfall than the County and the grass there is just as green. But it has dense mists too, and treacherous bogs. In the south-west there are also malevolent goat mages. We know more about them than we do about the witches—'

'I *do* remember reading about them!' I interrupted.

'Aye, the goat mages worship the Old God, Pan. They're a force to be reckoned with but never leave Ireland. As far as records go back, there is no mention of these Celtic witches visiting the County either. But amongst our fragments of knowledge is the name of the Old God they worship – the Morrigan. She haunts battlefields, and some call her the Goddess of

221

Slaughter. When summoned to this earth by one of the Celtic witches, she usually takes the shape of a large black crow—'

'The big crow on the branch?'

Arkwright shrugged. 'Who knows? But there's one more thing that I've heard said about Celtic witches. There are lots of burial mounds in Eire – and I mean a lot. For every one we have in the County, they have at least another ten. It's said that those witches can get into burial mounds and take refuge there. And that's exactly what she did when you chased her – I'm almost certain of it. I think we're dealing with a Celtic witch, Master Ward, and because we don't know much about her or her powers, that makes her *very* dangerous!'

Before going into the garden to keep watch, Arkwright decided to pay his respects to the mistress of the house again, so we went round to the tradesmen's entrance. This time it was a long while before anyone answered the door, and Arkwright started snorting with impatience.

The same maid answered, but this time she didn't meet our eyes and merely beckoned us inside. We were led not into the kitchen but towards the front of the house and were shown into a large drawing room.

Mistress Wicklow was standing with her back to the fire, her face pale; she was dressed in black. To her right, beneath the curtained window, was a coffin positioned on a long low table draped with a purple cloth. Two large candles were burning: one at its head, the other at its foot.

'My husband died suddenly last night at the very moment that the banshee wailed for the third time. Where were you?' she demanded, a dangerous chill to her voice.

'A child was killed by a worme and I was called away urgently,' Arkwright said abruptly, bending the truth a little. 'But I left my very capable apprentice here on watch. And from what he tells me, I don't think we are dealing with a banshee at all . . .'

Mistress Wicklow lowered her gaze to the carpet and her hands started to flutter nervously. She clasped them together tightly in an attempt to keep them still.

'Ah, I see it now. You knew that already, didn't you?' Arkwright accused her. 'You *knew* there was a witch out there . . .'

She looked up to meet his gaze, her eyes brimming with tears. 'We've been here in the County almost five years and I thought we were safe. But they've sent a witch assassin after us. She's killed my husband and I'll be next.'

'*They?* Who? A witch clan?' demanded Arkwright.

'No,' she said, shaking her head. 'Celtic witches don't form clans. They always work alone. The goat mages sent her. They want revenge for what my husband did. Do you know of those mages? Do you know what they do?'

'We know very little about them, ma'am. Most of what happens on that island of yours is a mystery to us.'

'Each year the mages tether a goat to a high platform,' she explained. 'They worship it for a week and a day. Human beings are sacrificed until the animal is gradually possessed by one of the Old Gods called Pan. Soon the goat starts to talk, stands upon its hind legs and grows larger, dominating the proceedings and demanding more and more sacrifices.'

What she was telling us was already in the Spook's Bestiary – Arkwright would also have read it there, but he let her speak without interruption in the hope of learning something new from a native of Ireland.

'The power they gain during those days of blood-shed lasts the goat mages for almost a year. But some years things go badly wrong. If Pan doesn't possess the goat, the mages must flee the region, taking refuge in hiding places throughout Ireland. They're vulnerable then, and their sworn enemies, a federation of landowners to the south-west, hunt them down. My husband was part of that federation; at that time, eight years ago, when the mages were weak, he was its leader. The landowners managed to kill five of them.

'But, following that, there was a succession of good years for the mages, when their power was in the ascendancy. Then it was their turn to hunt and kill the landowners. So, in fear for our lives, we gathered what we could of our wealth and fled here. This house belonged to my husband's brother, a bachelor. He died in a riding accident last year and my husband inherited it. We thought we were safe here, but the goat mages and the federation are in a perpetual state of war. Somehow our enemies found out where we were living and sent the witch after us.'

'If you knew, why didn't you tell us? My apprentice could have been killed!'

'I thought if you found out what you faced, you might not take on the job. I was scared and desperate.'

'What *do* we face, then? You come from that land. What powers does a Celtic witch have – especially an assassin?'

This really was an area we knew nothing about; more material for my notebook.

'They are deadly with blades and spears. Sometimes they impale their enemies so that they die slowly. But their favourite method is the one used against my husband – the one that will soon be employed against me. They mimic banshees – that's why my people call them banshee witches; though instead of just fore-telling a death, they bring it about. When they lift the burial shroud from the water and wring it out, by dark magic they twist the heart and arteries of their victim. Last night, when the witch wailed for the third time, my husband's heart burst and blood spurted from his mouth to saturate the pillow. Tonight she'll begin the process again. This time *I'll* be the victim.'

'Not if we can help it. But it may take us more than one night,' Arkwright said.

'You have until her third cry on the third night. Then, if you fail, I will also die.'

Arkwright nodded, then turned to leave the room. 'I'm sorry for your loss,' he said.

'He wasn't a nice man,' Mistress Wicklow told us, an edge of bitterness in her voice. 'Ours was a marriage arranged by our families. I never loved him. He was a fool and he caused me nothing but trouble.'

Arkwright bowed his head, at a loss for words.

'Have you eaten?' she asked us.

'We fast when we face the dark,' Arkwright answered. 'But we'd appreciate a light breakfast tomorrow morning. We'll need to keep up our strength for what's ahead.'

Mistress Wicklow rang for the maid, who showed us out through the tradesmen's entrance once more. We began to walk down the garden, heading towards the lake.

'Well, Master Ward,' Arkwright commented, keeping his voice low. 'This is something new all right. We face a Celtic witch, so ready your silver chain!'

CHAPTER 5
THE BANSHEE CRY

Once more we settled ourselves down on the narrow bridge. My silver chain was now in the left pocket of my breeches, and I coiled it about my wrist, ready to throw. We didn't have to wait long . . .

Soon the terrible wailing banshee cry echoed over the garden. This time it came from further round the lake, near the burial mound. Immediately Arkwright set off at a run; I followed close at his heels.

The second cry came far more quickly than it had the previous night. Would the witch shriek for the third time before we reached her? She did, and I groaned

229

inside. Mistress Wicklow would already have been hurt.

Arkwright was now on my right, almost level with me and running towards the source of the cry. 'There she is!' he called out, pointing with his staff as he ran. I saw a female figure ahead, fleeing through the trees.

Suddenly something dark swooped down towards me, claws outstretched. I ducked and glanced to my right as it glided on silently towards Arkwright. It was the large black crow I'd seen the previous night. I heard him cry out; saw him stumble.

'Keep going!' he shouted. 'Keep after her!'

I kept running, but the moon had gone behind a cloud and all that told me the witch was still ahead was the slap-slap of her bare feet against the ground. We were coming towards the end of the trees and the mound lay just beyond the wood. This time I felt sure that I was catching up with her. I prepared to throw my silver chain, relying on my ears to guide me.

All at once, straight ahead, there was an explosion of light so bright that it hurt my eyes. It was like gazing directly into the sun. My vision instantly darkened and I stumbled to a halt. The light quickly faded in intensity; now it was just the silver of a full moon, but one that had fallen to earth.

It wasn't the moon though; it was a circular door in the grassy wall of the burial mound. I could see the black silhouette of the banshee witch against it. As the light faded, I glimpsed things beyond, within the mound; what looked like a table and chairs . . .

It was dark once again and I walked slowly forward to face the mound. Now there was no sign of a door at all – just grass. The real moon came out again; I looked down and saw more footprints.

Arkwright ran to my side. There was a cut on his head, just above his left eye. Blood was running down his face.

'Are you all right?' I asked.

'It's nothing,' he growled. 'Bit of a scratch. That bird did it. Probably her familiar. So the witch got away again?'

I nodded. 'She did go into the mound – I'm sure of

it. I saw a door this time, a circular entrance, and things inside. Looked like furniture.'

'Furniture? You'll be telling me next that she's got a bed in there and is going to settle down for a cosy sleep. Sure you weren't seeing things, Master Ward?'

'It really did look like a table and chairs.'

'Well, the eyes can play funny tricks in such situations, but I am inclined to believe that by use of dark magic she's somehow taken refuge in that mound.'

We spent the rest of the night on the bridge, taking it in turns to sleep. Not that we expected anything to happen again that night, but Arkwright wasn't taking any chances.

At dawn we washed our faces and hands in the lake, then went back to the tradesmen's entrance once more.

'Your mistress promised us a bite of breakfast,' Arkwright told the maid.

We ate a light meal of bread, cheese and ham, and were then shown through to the drawing room again. Mistress Wicklow was sitting in an armchair in front of the fire, wrapped in a long shawl. She was shivering and her lips had a blue tinge.

'I've always had a fear of dying in my bed,' she said, her voice slightly breathless, 'so I prefer to sit in my chair until all this ends – one way or the other . . .'

'She escaped into the mound,' Arkwright explained. 'But don't you worry – she won't get away tonight.'

'You've hurt your face,' she observed.

'It was a black crow that seems to be around whenever the witch is – probably just her familiar. Though I reckon it *could* be the Morrigan. But if it really *is* her, I'd expect her to do more than just scratch my face . . .'

Mistress Wicklow shook her head. 'Not necessarily. They say that those who are cut or scratched by the Morrigan are marked for death. They always die within the year. Of course, that's probably just a foolish superstition – and it probably wasn't the goddess anyway.'

We thanked Mistress Wicklow for breakfast, took our leave of her and strolled back towards the lake. It was a nice day, but there was little warmth in the sun. It would be a long wait until nightfall. I just wanted to get all this over with and return to the mill.

'Quite a deep cut,' Arkwright said, kneeling down to gaze at his face in the mirror of the lake. 'Don't think it'll scar though. Wouldn't want it to spoil my good looks!'

I laughed.

He was on his feet in a flash and cuffed me hard across the back of the head, sending me reeling forward. I almost fell into the water.

'It's not *that* funny, Master Ward,' he said angrily. 'I'm your master and you're just the apprentice. I expect a little respect.'

'I thought you were making a joke!' I protested.

'Blood and bone!' he cursed. 'I was – but it was a very mild joke. You laughed too long and too loud.' He suddenly gave me a wolfish grin, showing a mouthful of teeth. 'Get yourself ready, Master Ward. We shouldn't neglect your training. Prepare to defend yourself!'

With that, he picked up his staff and attacked me, trying to drive me into the lake. We fought for almost an hour, and by the end of it, muscles I didn't know I had were complaining and I'd two more bruises to add to my collection. But Arkwright never did manage to force me into the lake, so that counted as some sort of victory.

'We'll do things differently tonight,' he said as we rested on the bridge once more. 'You chase her towards the mound. I'll lie in wait amongst the trees close to it and block her escape.'

It seemed a good plan – that is, if the witch didn't somehow manage to long-sniff the threat. Witches could usually do this to see danger coming. But as seventh sons of seventh sons, spooks were usually immune to this power – though with a witch about whom we knew little, nothing was certain.

That night, the first cry of the banshee witch told me that she was very close! This time she had further to run in order to reach the safety of the mound. I might even be able to catch her before the edge of the wood. So, putting my silver chain in my pocket and gripping my staff, I ran towards the sound.

There was often an edge of competition between my temporary master and me; it would be really pleasing to bind her with my chain before he could intercept her, I thought. So I ran just as fast as I could in the direction of the cry. She would hear me coming, but I didn't care. I was on the attack. My heart was pounding and I was filled with exhilaration.

The second cry came very soon after the first. The witch would be using some kind of curse that demanded a precise form of words. Surely there had to be a limit to how fast she could utter it? But, to my dismay, the third cry echoed over the lake before I reached her. I groaned, remembering Mistress Wicklow's blue-tinged lips and breathlessness. Now she would have suffered further pain.

I drove myself on even harder. I could hear the witch running through the trees ahead. I *had* to catch her. We hadn't managed to stop her uttering her third cry tonight – what chance had we of doing that tomorrow, when it would kill her victim? I wondered.

I could see her just ahead of me now and I was closing fast, readying my silver chain. As I was about to cast it, she swerved to the left so that a tree lay between me and my target.

Suddenly a burly figure rose up to confront her. Arkwright! They seemed to collide . . . he fell . . . she staggered and ran on. We were in the open now, beyond the trees, making straight for the mound. Just as I was about to cast my chain, the light blazed out again. Again I was blinded, but this time I kept going. The witch's silhouette came into view against the round yellow doorway. Then, all at once, darkness and silence.

For a moment I didn't realize what had happened. The air was warmer and absolutely still. Lights flared on the rocky walls – I saw black candles in brackets. And furniture! My eyes hadn't deceived me. There was a small table and two wooden straight-backed chairs. I was inside the burial mound!

I'd followed the witch through the magical door, and there she was, standing directly ahead of me, still gripping the rolled-up burial shroud, an expression of anger and bemusement on her face. I took a few deep breaths to calm myself and slow my pounding heart.

'What a fool you be, to follow me!' cried the witch.

'Do you always talk in rhyme?' I asked.

The witch didn't reply because, as I spoke, I cast my silver chain and it brought her to her knees, the links tight against her mouth to silence her. It was a perfect shot. I'd bound the witch – but now I had a real problem . . .

There was no visible door. How was I going to get out of the mound?

I searched the inside of the chamber carefully, running my fingers over the place where I thought I'd entered, but it was seamless. I was in a rocky cave without an entrance. Arkwright was on the outside; I was trapped inside. Had I bound the witch – or had she bound *me*? I looked at her. She was still gripping the shroud; despite the chain she hadn't dropped it.

I knelt close to her, staring into her eyes, which seemed to crinkle with amusement. Beneath the chain her mouth was pulled away from her teeth; half smile, half grimace. But her face wasn't that of the hideous hag I'd glimpsed as she washed the shroud. It could have belonged to any young country woman passed without a second glance at a market. Perhaps she'd used some spell to try and scare me off – a mild form of *dread* perhaps?

I eased the chain from her mouth so that she could speak. It was a dangerous thing to do, but I urgently needed to question her; make her tell me how I could get out. But I soon realized that it was a big mistake . . .

Her lips free of the chain, the witch was free to speak dark magic spells, and she began to do that immediately. She uttered three quick phrases, each in a language I'd never heard before, each ending in a rhyme. Then she opened her mouth very wide, and a thick black cloud of smoke erupted from it.

I sprang to my feet and staggered backwards. The cloud continued to grow – to the point where her whole face was engulfed. It reminded me of the blood from the shroud that had stained the water of the lake. Now the air between us grew dark and tainted.

The cloud was becoming even denser and taking on a shape. There were wings. Outstretched claws. A ravenous beak. It had become a black crow. The witch's open mouth was a portal to the dark! It was the Morrigan!

But this was no longer a bird of normal size and proportions; it was nothing like the seemingly ordinary crow that had swooped through the trees to attack Bill Arkwright. This creature was immense; it was distorted and twisted into something grotesque. The beak, legs and claws were elongated, stretching out towards me, while the head and body remained relatively small.

But then the wings grew too, until they reached out on either side of the monstrous bird to fill all the available space. They flapped violently, battering against the walls of the chamber and smashing the table so that it broke in half. Its claws struck out at me. I ducked and they raked the wall over my head, gouging deep grooves into the rock.

For a moment I was filled with panic. A spook has little chance of defeating one of the Old Gods. I was going to die here, I was sure. But then I took a deep breath and calmed myself. My master had taught me well, and I knew that the first and most important thing to do was control my fear. I'd faced great dangers from the dark before and survived. I could do so again . . .

So I concentrated hard, feeling the strength rise within me. And confidence began to replace fear. There was anger too.

I acted without conscious decision, with a speed that astonished even me. I stepped forward, closer to the Morrigan, released the retractable blade and swept my staff across from left to right. The blade cut deep into the bird's breast, slicing a bloody red line through the black feathers.

There was a tremendous scream. The Morrigan convulsed and contracted, shrinking rapidly until she was no larger than my fist. Then she vanished – leaving behind only a few black feathers smeared with blood that fluttered slowly to the ground.

The witch shook her head, her expression one of acute astonishment. 'That's not possible!' she cried. 'Who are you to be able to do such a thing?'

'My name is Tom Ward,' I told her. 'I'm a spook's apprentice and my job is to fight the dark.'

She smiled grimly. 'Well, you've fought your last fight, boy. There is no way you can escape this place. Soon the goddess will return. You will not find it so easy a second time.'

I smiled and looked down at the blood-splattered feathers littering the floor. Then I looked up and stared her straight in the eye, doing my best not to blink. 'We'll see. Next time I might cut off her head . . .'

I was bluffing, of course; trying to appear more confident than I felt. I had to persuade this witch to open the door of the mound.

'You're a fool, boy. She'll return, slay you, then carry off your soul to her kingdom in the dark!'

'In that case you may suffer the same fate!' I warned. 'You brought her into a dangerous situation that caused her pain. She might feel that should earn its own reward . . .'

I watched expressions flicker across the witch's face: anger, uncertainty, and then fear. The Old Gods could be vindictive and vengeful, even towards their own servants. There was some truth in what I'd just said, and the witch knew it.

'So why don't you open the door so that we can leave this mound?' I continued.

'What? So that you can kill me or bind me for ever? Which fate do you have in store for me?'

'Neither. Once outside I'll release you from the chain. But, in return, you must promise to stop cursing Mistress Wicklow and go back to Ireland.'

'Why worry about her? She and her man were landowners who cared nothing at all for their servants and tenants. Six years ago, when the crops failed, they let the people starve. They could have helped but they didn't . . .'

'I know nothing about that. But you've killed her husband. Isn't that enough?' I asked.

The witch frowned, but then she allowed the shroud to fall from her left hand to the floor. 'Help me to my feet!' she commanded.

I did as she asked, and she hobbled towards the rock wall and muttered words in the same strange language as before. There was a flare of pale light and the doorway opened before us. Gripping the chain, I pulled her forward into the cold night air. The moon bathed the mound behind us in silver light.

'Release me!' she commanded.

'Will you keep your word?'

'Yes, but will *you* keep yours?'

I nodded and, with a flick of my wrist, released

JOSEPH DELANEY

the witch from the chain. She smiled. 'Don't ever visit my land, boy. The Morrigan is much more powerful there. And she is vengeful. She would torment you beyond anything you can imagine. Whatever you do, stay away from Ireland.'

With that, the banshee witch turned her back on me and made a sign in the air, muttering under her breath. Beyond her, the door faded and became the sheer grassy wall of the burial mound.

I think she was about to turn back and say something to me, but she never got the chance.

Something flew through the air towards her and buried itself between her shoulder blades. She fell down in the mud, a knife buried to the hilt in her back. She groaned, twitched twice and lay still.

Bill Arkwright walked towards me from the edge of the trees, carrying his staff and bag.

'You did a deal with her, Master Ward? Can't blame you, I suppose. How else could you have got out of that mound?'

'She would have kept her promise!' I protested.

'She was going home. She wasn't going to complete the curse . . .'

'You've just the word of a witch for that,' Arkwright said. 'What I've just done makes things more certain. Now she *can't* complete the curse. Am I right?'

'But I gave her my word—'

'Blood and bone!' cursed Arkwright. 'Grow up, boy! This is what we do. We kill witches. We fight the dark. If you can't stomach the job, go back to your farm!'

I didn't speak. I just stared down at the dead witch.

'What's done is done,' said Arkwright, pulling the knife out of her back. 'If you're squeamish, don't linger here . . .'

So I walked back through the trees and waited for him on the bridge. Dead witches could scratch their way to the surface of their graves and go hunting for victims. He was cutting out her heart to make sure that she couldn't come back.

* * *

We went to see Mistress Wicklow, and Arkwright told her most of what had happened. She seemed even more breathless than the previous night, but felt confident that she'd now make a full recovery. My master told her where the dead witch was, and she made arrangements to have her buried close to the mound. Then she paid him and we took our leave of her.

We walked back to the mill in silence. I was far from happy with what had happened and couldn't bring myself to chat to Arkwright; he too seemed lost in his own thoughts.

At last we waded through the salt moat that protects his garden from water witches and other creatures of the dark, and headed for the side door. Before we reached it, Claw started to bark.

'Well, at least somebody's speaking to me!' Arkwright said. But when we went in, Claw didn't bound towards him as I'd expected. She was otherwise occupied . . .

'Good girl! Good girl!' Arkwright said, kneeling down to pat her on the head.

She was feeding her new-born pups. There were two of them.

'So what shall we call these two little beauties, Master Ward?'

I smiled. 'Blood and Bone?' I suggested.

Arkwright grinned up at me. 'Perfect!' he exclaimed. 'Couldn't have chosen better myself. That's what I'll call them.'

The pups had stopped feeding now. Arkwright got to his feet and reached down into his bag. 'Better safe than sorry,' he said. 'And a nice treat for a new mother!'

Then he pulled out the witch's heart and threw it to Claw.

I had other adventures with Bill Arkwright, but that's the one I'll never forget. It's because of what Mistress Wicklow said: that those cut or scratched by the Morrigan are marked for death – they always die within the year.

And Bill Arkwright did die less than a year later,

sacrificing his life in Greece so that the Spook, Alice and I could escape.

Perhaps we paid a high price for dealing with that banshee witch.

THE SPOOK'S SERIES

WARNING:
NOT TO BE READ AFTER DARK

Joseph Delaney is a retired English teacher living in Lancashire. He has three children and nine grandchildren, and often speaks at all sorts of events. His home is in the middle of boggart territory and his village has a boggart called the Hall Knocker, which was laid to rest under the step of a house near the church.

Most of the places in the Spook's books are based on real locations in Lancashire, and the inspiration behind them often comes from local ghost stories and legends.

You can visit the *Wardstone Chronicles* website at www.**spooksbooks**.com where you can find Joseph's blog and more information on the books.